THROUGH MY OWN LENS

Horizons, Book Five

Mickie B. Ashling

Acknowledgements

I'd like to thank my friend Jeannie, as well as my awesome beta readers, for helping me bring this story to life. A big shout-out to my publisher, Raevyn McCann, for taking a chance on characters that are already part of an established series.

Author's Note

Six-year-old Luca Dilorio made his first appearance in my novel *Taste* in 2011. Since then, he's become a beloved character in the Horizons Series. In my novel *Chyna Doll,* fifteen-year-old Luca struggles with his orientation and his growing feelings for Chyna Davidson, a complex character who has faced and overcome many challenges, having been born intersex to a family in denial.

Through My Own Lens is a coming-of-age novel, part two of Luca and Chyna's journey. Deeply in love, the high school graduates head for the East Coast. Chyna embarks on his modeling career in Manhattan while Luca enrolls at Cornell in Ithaca, New York. Learning how to function as separate entities after being a unit for years presents obstacles neither one anticipates. Roommates Zeb Araneda and Alex Boulet, new additions to the series, help the struggling couple figure it out.

I've been warned that family dramas aren't a thing in the m/m genre. Supposedly, most readers won't take the time to catch up on a long-standing series, but I believe a properly constructed story will include enough history to make it shine as a standalone. I'm hoping this is the case with *Through My Own Lens*. You can enjoy the next chapter of Luca and Chyna's story without reading the previous books—unless you want to.

Catch up on Zeb and Alex sometime in the near future by following my blog for updates on my writing and other news.

www.mickiebashling.blogspot.com

Chapter One

LOWERING HIS CAMERA, Ian Carmichael squinted across the divide of harsh lights and eviscerated me with one question. "Do you always look like this, or did someone come in your mouth without your permission?"

Stunned by the unexpected attack, I struggled to catch my breath while deliberating my next move. I could throat punch the asshole—and get on the blacklist—or choose the high road and keep my dignity intact.

"Don't just stand there, Red. Answer me when I ask you something."

My pulse sped up, and I was tempted to walk out the door, but that would only prove I was an incompetent newbie. I decided to tough it out, but not until I had my say.

"First off, my name is Chyna Davidson, not Red, and you might consider rephrasing your question."

Instead of backing down, Ian challenged. "What the hell kind of name is Chyna anyway?"

"Not that it's any of your business, but my mother was a fan of Wilson Phillips."

"Who?"

"Forget it." *Clueless motherfucker.*

"Listen up, kiddo. Once you've attained supermodel status, you can patent that insouciance, but at the moment, you're nothing but a wannabe. Start making love to my camera or find another career."

"Sorry?"

"Jesus fucking Christ!" Ian roared. "Pretend I'm your boyfriend and you're craving some attention."

Ooh, that did it. Yelling had never worked with me, and unfiltered words projected out of my mouth like vomit. "Dude, I have a boyfriend, and he gives me plenty of attention. And just so we're clear, I'm not your bitch, so get over yourself. Fame doesn't give you the right to be a first-class prick. You. Chose. Me. Stop acting like a bully and tell me what to do without insulting me."

"Give me a goddamn break." Ian turned his back and reached for one of several bottles of water he kept on the table piled high with camera lenses and filters. He drained the liquid in a few gulps while I stared at his backside, which, I had to admit, filled his faded jeans rather nicely. The world-renowned photographer, who'd begged for a fresh face to represent Armani's next spring collection, knew damn well what he was getting when he requested my presence. I never said I was experienced, and instead of treating me with compassion, he was being an utter jerk.

Ian hollered for Melinda, my agent, who appeared at his side within seconds. She and her husband, Dan, owned Elite Plus, the Chicago-based agency who'd first discovered me.

"What's the matter?" she asked, rubbing Ian's back gently.

"Do something with your boy or get me a replacement."

Hell no. I gnawed at my lower lip, terrified by the prospect of being fired on my first day of work. Ian was the most famous photog in Manhattan, the best of the best, or so I'd been told, and he wasn't too hard on the eyes if one was into silver foxes, which I wasn't, but that was beside the point. Making a good impression was the right move if I hoped to conquer the fashion world, but so far, this meeting had been a disaster. Ian tossed the empty bottle into a recycling bin and continued to glare at Melinda.

"I'm aware you have a deadline," she conceded softly, "but honestly, Ian, a little sugar would go a long way to make this easier on our collective nerves. You wouldn't have asked for Chyna if you didn't believe he had potential."

"I don't have time to babysit," he snapped.

"No one's asking you to feed and burp the guy," Melinda argued. "Chyna's a natural, but he doesn't know you or what you're hoping to achieve. You'd get a lot more cooperation if you encouraged rather than criticized."

"My God, woman! Do you have any idea how long it's been since anyone asked *me* to adjust my attitude? I'm not the one with a problem. It's your brat who needs a swift kick in the ass."

I could feel my anger—and humiliation—rising again. My hands curled into fists as I got ready to punch Ian's lights out.

"You're the one acting like a diva," Melinda shot back. "Chyna's a hard worker with a lot of potential star power. It's up to you to unleash the magic, not snuff it out with your craptastic posturing."

Ian's mouth gaped. I wondered how long it would take security to escort us out of the studio, and I was surprised—honestly flabbergasted—when it didn't happen.

"Okay," Ian agreed, backing down. "I'm willing to give this another chance, but I want to see more sass and less pouting."

Nodding, Melinda acknowledged his request with a curt "Got it."

She covered the short distance between us in a few determined strides, and I braced for whatever was coming next. Mel was fired up, willing to go the extra mile to ensure my success, but the responsibility now rested squarely on my shoulders. If I didn't live up to her hype, I might as well pack it up.

My family would probably be relieved if I walked away, but Mel's reputation was on the line, and I owed her big-time. When I walked into Elite Plus four years ago, I'd been passing for female, due in part to being born intersex, but mainly because of my mother's irrational desire to have a daughter. Against all medical advice, and despite my fully formed male genitalia, she'd been raising me as a girl. Mel had seen through the charade and gently coaxed me into becoming my authentic self. She was more than my agent—she was my mentor and best friend. I couldn't let her down after she'd put her reputation on the line for me.

"What an asshole," I muttered. "He's obviously too full of himself to mentor anyone."

"I won't deny it," Mel whispered, "but Ian's very much in demand. You're lucky to be here."

"Seriously?"

"Hon, you'll have to trust me on this."

"Any suggestions?"

"Put some enthusiasm into your smiles," she began, "and own your beauty."

"Sorry, but it's difficult when he acts like I'm a waste of time."

Mel gave me the look she usually reserved for gossipy tidbits. "He'll never admit it, but I know Ian finds you attractive, and that's a big plus right there."

"How can you tell?"

"His nostrils flared when we walked in."

Grinning, I turned in his direction and noticed him watching us. I quickly looked away. "He must be a Taurus or something."

Mel smirked. "I've heard he's hung like a bull."

"Gross. Weren't you the one who said a huge cock was overrated?"

"If it's being shoved up my hole, but I never said they weren't fun to look at," she finished with a wink.

"He's too old anyway."

"Hon, he's only thirty-nine. I know that in your nineteen-year-old world that's ancient, but he's actually a man in his prime."

"Regardless," I muttered. "He's an insensitive pig."

"Now's not the time to assert yourself, Chyna. Give him what he wants, and when you get to the point where designers are fighting over you, then you can tell him to kiss your ass."

"You honestly think he'll be more cooperative after your lecture?"

"I do," Mel nodded. "Now turn on the awesomeness."

She returned to her side of the room to watch me do my thing.

I did my best to get into a better headspace by thinking of Luca. Ian wasn't too far off the mark with that suggestion. My boyfriend's mixed heritage—Italian and Filipino—had blended perfectly, producing a black-haired, doe-eyed stud with the most kissable mouth this side of the Atlantic. Melinda was dying to represent him and had begged him to pose for a few head shots, but Luca always refused. He wanted to be an architect and join the Chicago-based firm founded by Lil Lampert, his stepfather, and his dad, Grier Dilorio. Someday it would be Lampert, Dilorio & Son, which was why Luca was in Ithaca instead of observing my photo shoot.

The issue of college had been debated over the last eighteen months. Lil had pushed for Stanford, his Alma Mater, but Luca reminded his stepfather that Cornell had a great architectural program, and it was closer to Manhattan than Palo Alto would ever be. Staying close to me had been Luca's main objective, and there was nothing anyone could say to change his mind. Thank fuck. I didn't know what I'd have done if he'd caved and gone West. Chip, my twin, and Luca's best friend, had stayed in Illinois. He and his girlfriend, Meghan, were enrolled at Northwestern University. They'd been a couple throughout high school, and we all knew they'd go to the same college. They planned to marry before he moved on to med school.

The immediate concern—mine and everyone else's—was seeing if I was going to make it as a model or join Luca at Cornell, where I'd taken a one-year deferment. I was finally standing in front of a camera after delaying my career for a couple of reasons. I had to finish high school, for one thing, and, more importantly, I needed to come to grips with my gender dysphoria. My foster parents—who were best friends with Luca's parents—hadn't been comfortable sending me off to New York on my own until my issues were thoroughly resolved. Through months of intense therapy, and Luca's support, thoughts of transitioning to female were slowly being put to rest. I'd been living life as a male for the last three years, and getting used to it, mostly, but like everything else in my convoluted life, embracing my authentic self was a work in progress.

Now and then, I'd fall back into femme mode, applying makeup, slipping on a silky chemise, and pulling up lace panties rather than boxers. At first, the incidents left me confused, so I stomped on the urge, but when Luca assured me that it wasn't a problem and, in fact, he found it *sexy as hell,* I put a lid on my fears and embraced that side of my nature. For fifteen years, I'd been pretending I was female, and short of having a lobotomy, I couldn't forget the simple pleasure I derived from satin, eye shadow, and high heels.

Casting off all fears of rejection had been the biggest plus in my newly formed world. Luca had fallen for me when I was posing as female, and when it was revealed—in the ugliest most dramatic way possible—that I had a penis, and not the vagina he'd been expecting, Luca reassured me that his love went beyond body parts. It had been a defining moment in my life, and the unconditional support I'd received from the people that mattered the most had enabled me to move past the shame. I stepped into my new role as Luca's boyfriend and Barrington High School's first male cheerleader with pride.

The major problem these days was finding the time and place to meet. Aside from geographical constraints, there were work and school commitments to contend with. Both of us were overachievers. I wanted to prove modeling was a good fit for me, and Luca had to figure out how to balance school, football, and our relationship. Something would suffer if we didn't learn how to manage our time.

Future goals aside, we were totally bummed out by our first separation in four years. Since the beginning of high school, we'd seen each other almost every day. Finding private time hadn't been easy, but we'd managed a few special moments once we worked out parental schedules. This current separation was going on four weeks, and it felt like an eternity. Phone sex had been fun in the beginning, but it was getting old. I was perpetually horny, and right then, the idea of sex with

Luca sent a signal straight to my cock. Heat crept up my neck and my cheeks felt like they were on fire. Adjusting myself, I caught Ian staring at my crotch and smirking.

"Thinking of your man does great things to your complexion," he leered.

"Shut up." I was mortified for being called out.

Ian hooted. "Did I hit it on the nail?"

I flipped him the bird but couldn't hide my smile.

"Jesus, you're gorgeous when you drop the mask," Ian muttered to himself as the camera whirred and clicked a zillion shots per second. "Shake your hair out, kiddo, and look dazzling."

I raked my long hair with both hands, the one constant in my ever-changing world. Luca loved my hair, twirling the strands around his fingers when we talked or tugging on my ponytail to get my attention. Ian seemed to dig redheads as well. It was empowering, and the idea of reducing the snarky photographer into my lapdog gave me a small measure of satisfaction. Ian circled, angling the camera to get a better shot, coming close one minute and backing up the next.

"Take off your tie," he purred. "Unbutton your shirt so I can see some of that fuzz."

I did as I was told, in slow motion of course, moving my gaze down Ian's body and resting them on the bulge that had grown more noticeable in the last ten minutes. I licked my lips and Ian went nuts.

"That's it, kiddo. Look at me and say 'do me' like you mean it."

That made me pause. Should I object or go with the flow now that peace had been restored? His suggestion made me feel dirty, and I was tempted to shoot him down, but I let it slide. Next time Ian crossed the line, I'd knee him in the nuts.

After what seemed like hours, the camera stopped whirring, and Ian gave me an enthusiastic nod of approval. "You rock, kiddo. Let's go and have a drink to celebrate."

"I'm not legal."

"Right," he said, chuckling. "How about if you have a virgin *whatever* while Melinda and I have our grownup drinks?"

"Nice. Just when I thought you were a decent guy, you had to go and fuck it up with that comment."

Ian snorted. "Don't worry, Chyna. I'm a regular at the bar, and it won't be a problem to slip you a beer."

"Actually, I don't like the taste of beer."

"We'll find something you do like." Ian promised.

"Okay." Maybe modeling wasn't that hard when you had the photog eating out of your hand. With success on my mind, and nothing else, I agreed to join him and Mel.

"I have to pass," Melinda said. "But you should go with Ian."

I'd known Mel long enough to know she wanted me to accept the invitation and continue bonding with Mr. Wonderful. The photo shoot had ended on a high note, and sealing our partnership with a friendly drink must have been SOP in the industry. Refusing him would be tantamount to saying I didn't trust him. I hesitated for another second, and I could see panic written all over Mel's face. Hopefully Luca wouldn't flip out when I recounted my day. He had a jealous streak a mile wide, but this was my business, and staying on Ian's good side could only mean better jobs in the future.

"Okay," I decided. "Lead the way."

"Great," he said, giving me the first genuine smile since I'd met him. Mel seemed relieved by my decision and promised to call me later.

Ian took me to a bar about five blocks away, and after we got settled, he ordered a salty dog for himself and a tequila sunrise for me. My fruity beverage came in a tall glass with an orange slice and cherry stuck to the rim. I chowed down the garnish because I was ravenous, and when I took my first sip of the drink, I was relieved the booze was masked by the tangy orange juice. If I had been savvier, I would have nursed my drink, instead of gulping it down like a thirsty camel, but that's exactly what I didn't do. Ian lifted his hand when my glass was empty and a fresh drink appeared out of nowhere. This time they added a plate of cut-up bagel dogs and mini pizzas. I pounced on the food and shoved an entire pizza in my mouth.

Ian raised a brow. "Hungry much?"

Embarrassed, I tried explaining around a mouthful of cheesy dough. "Haven't eaten anything since breakfast."

"Neither have I," Ian said, "but I'm used to it. You'll soon learn that a proper breakfast, with the right amount of protein and carbs, is what will carry you through the day. Lunches are a rare event in our industry. I don't want you to fall back on coffee and cigarettes like most of your peers. Malnutrition will make you break out, and it'll add years to your appearance. It's not a good look on anyone, especially a model."

"Is that a common thing in this industry?" I asked, reaching for a bagel dog. I'd been blessed with a great metabolism and could usually eat anything I wanted without gaining an ounce.

"Eating disorders are rampant," Ian said with a moue of disgust, "as well as alcohol and drug abuse. You have to work on your inner strength to keep those demons at bay."

"I'm not addicted to anything," I pronounced. "You don't have to worry about me."

"What about success?" Ian asked.

I stopped midchew and blinked at him.

"The need to be number one is also an addiction, Chyna. People do crazy things to get ahead. Learn how to find the right balance, or you'll crash and burn."

"Right," I said, drawing out the word. He was staring at me like he could see into my soul. If Ian only knew the shit I'd overcome to get to this point, he'd realize I *would* do anything to succeed in this world.

After stuffing my face, I'd sobered up enough to risk taking the subway home, even though Ian suggested Uber. I didn't want him to think I was a lightweight. Despite our rocky start, I could tell he had years of wisdom to impart, and once the snarky prima donna was put aside, he wasn't so bad. His opinion mattered, and I intended to stay on his good side.

We bro-hugged at the top of the subway entrance, and he walked away without a backward glance. I headed down the stairs, jostling with hundreds of tired commuters, determined to get a seat for the twenty-minute ride uptown. Luck was on my side, and I was able to slide into a chair as soon as I stepped on. I stuck in my earbuds and started my playlist. It was always the same set, the ones they'd played the night of my senior prom. Memories of that special time materialized with each song, and as I listened to Justin Bieber, Taylor Swift, and Rihanna. I closed my eyes and remembered.

Chapter Two

LUCA PACED AS much as one could in a small dorm room. He would have been better off running a few laps to get rid of some of this nervous energy, but he'd been waiting ages for Chyna to return his texts, and he couldn't concentrate for shit. With his luck, he'd trip over his own feet, and that would defeat the purpose. Exercise was supposed to relieve stress, not add to it. It was almost six in the evening, way past the time most people quit work, or didn't the rule apply to models?

Supporting Chyna's endeavors when it was a distant ambition was one thing, but now that dreams were finally starting to happen, he wasn't sure he could handle the abrupt shift from high school sweethearts to long-distance lovers. The thought of anyone touching, looking, or even talking to Chyna in his absence was giving Luca a tension headache.

Ever since he and Chyna began dating, way back in their freshman year of high school, he'd developed a protective streak that was oftentimes out of control and even embarrassing. He'd talked to his dads about it on several occasions, and the advice he'd received was heartfelt and sensible, but it didn't stop the surge of emotions that swamped him when he imagined Chyna getting manhandled.

They'd all witnessed Chyna's shame the day he'd been attacked at the Homecoming dance. It was a scene seared into Luca's memory, and no amount of brain bleach would wipe away the vision of Chyna's pain and humiliation as he stood with his bodice crumpled around his waist, so the entire student body could see the lengths he'd taken to pass himself off as female. Luca had vowed to protect him at all costs from any future attacks, and he'd succeeded for three years. But now things were different. The playing field had changed and he wasn't in control anymore. There was no telling what kind of trouble would surface without his constant vigilance.

Melinda had assured him that Chyna would be in a safe environment, and future roommates would be carefully screened, but until he saw them with his own eyes and talked to them to make sure they weren't homophobes or generally weird, he wouldn't stop worrying.

And speaking of roommates, his needed a reality check. Zeb Araneda seemed nice enough, but he'd never lived outside the Philippines, until now, and didn't know the first thing about dorm life. They'd made good progress with unpacking, but there were still a few stragglers, mostly Zeb's, blocking the path to the door. As an only child for many years, Luca had never shared a room. He wasn't sure if he could handle it or not, but he sure as heck knew they'd have to lay out some ground rules or he and Zeb would get on each other's nerves. More than likely it would be Luca who lost it.

"You think you can tackle the rest of your stuff before tomorrow?" Luca asked.

"Sure," Zeb said. "I don't suppose you'd be willing to help me?"

Luca studied Zeb. "What's the matter? Can't function without your maids?"

"You know how it is back home," Zeb muttered.

"Only secondhand," Luca said. "When Mom and my sister, Gemma, come back from visiting family in Manila, they act like a pair of spoiled princesses for a while."

"Hey, it's a part of our culture," Zeb defended.

"Regardless," Luca said, "you're here now and you'll have to learn to fend for yourself."

"They mentioned you were half Filipino, but no one warned me about the OCD."

Luca blinked, trying to see himself from Zeb's point of view. Immediately, he regretted his behavior. "I'm sorry if I'm coming on too strong, but I think it's better to get this out in the open. I don't have OCD, but I can't function in chaos. If you'll pick up after yourself, there won't be a problem. Understanding your culture doesn't make me more sympathetic."

"Noted," Zeb replied. "Now can we put a lid on the lecture and get something to eat?"

Luca slung an arm over Zeb's shoulder. "Sure, Z. Lead the way."

They were staying in one of the high-rises on Cornell's North Campus. There were several students hanging out in the central lounge when Luca and Zeb exited their room and headed toward the elevator.

"Later, dudes," Zeb said to no one in particular.

A chorus of grunts followed them down the hallway.

They ended up at Bear Necessities, a combination convenience store and grill located at the Robert Purcell Community Center. They didn't say much while they were devouring their food—double bacon cheeseburgers and a mountain of fries. Afterward, Zeb leaned forward and was about to say something, but Luca's phone finally buzzed. He smiled when he saw Chyna's face light up the screen.

"I've got to take this call," he informed Zeb.

"No prob."

Excited, Luca pushed back his chair and moved off to the other side of the room for privacy.

"Hey, you," he greeted Chyna warmly. "How's it going?"

"I miss you."

"Shit," Luca said, sighing. "I do too. Bad day?"

"Tiring. I've been at a photo shoot for the last six hours, and the asshole photographer gave me the stink eye each time I reached for my phone. That's why I didn't pick up."

"Who is this piece of shit?" Luca demanded.

"Some famous dude who rules the fashion world."

"Does he have a name so I can look him up?"

"Ian Carmichael," Chyna replied. "He and God are on a first-name basis from what I understand."

"Sounds like a douche," Luca commented.

"I thought so in the beginning, but he turned out to be okay. After we were done, he bought me drinks and some food at a bar a few blocks over."

"Are you kidding me?"

"Babe, chill. He was trying to make amends for being a turd."

"What sort of drinks?"

"Tequila Sunrise."

Luca started. "Weren't you carded?"

"Relax, will you? Ian's a regular and nobody questioned him or me."

"And that makes it right?"

"Maybe not, but it was exactly what I needed after our long day."

"How'd you get home? Weren't you buzzed?"

Chyna's loud sigh made Luca flinch and his follow-up statement felt like a slap.

"You weren't here, so stop being judgey. I did what I had to do."

"I hope this doesn't become a regular thing," Luca warned.

"Prolly not," Chyna ventured. "Today was my first day of work, and it was nice to be rewarded after I was able to turn things around. So, yeah, celebrating was the right thing to do."

Luca didn't appreciate the lecture, but he bit back his objections. There would be time enough in the future to revisit this conversation. "What are you doing now?"

"Lying down with my feet up on the wall."

"I'd give you a foot rub if I were there," Luca said sympathetically.

"There are other more important body parts that could use some rubbing."

Luca groaned loudly. "Don't get me started. I'll be there on Saturday, and since I have Monday off, we'll have three full days."

"Why do you have Monday off?"

"Labor Day," Luca stated.

"I forgot."

"It's easy when you're busy," Luca commiserated.

"What time will you get here?"

"If I catch the 5:30 a.m. bus, I'll be there in time to take you to breakfast," Luca said enthusiastically.

"Babe, you don't have to wake up at the crack of dawn."

"Never mind that," Luca said. "What's important is I'm going to be there on Saturday."

"I can hardly wait."

"No roommates yet?" Luca inquired.

"I'm interviewing a couple of people tomorrow."

"Don't have them move in until Monday or later," Luca advised.

"Why?"

"Duh."

"I'll have my own room, Luca. We'll always have privacy."

"I'd rather our first time in a month be completely solo. I can't promise I'll be quiet."

"Right?"

Luca could tell Chyna was smiling, and he was relieved they'd moved past the brief clash of wills. "I love you," he said softly. "So much."

"Me too. I can't wait to see you."

"Bye." He disconnected and returned to the table.

Zeb gave him a questioning look. "All good?"

"Yup," Luca said. "We're hooking up on Saturday."

"He's coming here?"

"Nah. I'm heading to Manhattan for the long weekend. How about you?"

Zeb shrugged. "I'm not sure yet."

"Do you have any family or friends in the area?"

"I have some cousins who live in Queens."

"Why not call them and ask if you can visit? We can take the same bus into the city."

"Good idea," Zeb said, nodding. "Thanks, man."

"For what?" Luca asked.

"Watching my back," Zeb replied. "It's nice of you to worry about me."

Luca was surprised by Zeb's gratitude. He was only being friendly after all. Now he was doubly remorseful for his stupid comments. Lumping Zeb into the same category as Gemma, his prepubescent sister, was totally out of line.

"We're roomies," Luca said in a conciliatory tone. "Got to stick together."

"You got that right," Zeb replied, flashing a toothy grin.

THE ENTHUSIASM HE'D tamped down for the past few days rushed to the forefront when he caught sight of Chyna waiting for him by the gate outside the Cornell Club. Even with a backward baseball cap hiding part of his hair, he was easy to spot in a crowd. Taller than most of the pedestrians scurrying alongside of him, Chyna's unguarded smile lit up his face, and Luca felt the familiar zing of excitement.

Instead of waiting in line to exit through the front, Luca slipped out the back door and dropped his backpack at Chyna's feet. They embraced, oblivious to the people streaming past them. Neither wore a jacket and it was much easier to feel the soft skin already rippling with goose bumps when Luca snuck his hands underneath Chyna's T.

Chyna pressed his hips against Luca's. "I've missed you," he whispered huskily.

Luca moaned when he felt the unmistakable proof. "How far to your place?"

"Seven stops on the Seventh Avenue Line."

"Let's go," he said, taking Chyna's hand and tugging him along.

"Wait. What about that guy?"

"Guy?"

"The one who hasn't stopped staring at us," Chyna said, inclining his head toward Zeb.

"Oh shit," Luca exclaimed. "That's my roommate."

"Is he coming too?"

"No, he's going to Queens. Here, let me introduce you."

They met halfway, and Zeb had to raise his head to look into Chyna's eyes.

"Zeb, this is Chyna."

"Nice to meet you."

"Same here," Chyna replied.

"You guys are gonna give me a stiff neck," Zeb observed, looking from Luca to Chyna.

"Can't help it if you're so short," Luca teased.

"Hey, I'm five nine. That's above average where I come from."

"Is it?" Luca asked.

"Don't mind him," Chyna said. "He's giving you a hard time."

"Am not," Luca said, grinning.

"You're a shit, Dilorio," Zeb said. "Your boyfriend's way nicer than you."

"Thanks, Zeb," Chyna said. "For a long time, I was insecure about my height. In school, I always felt like a crane among a flock of penguins, but then I realized it was a plus if I wanted to make it as a model. My agent couldn't have been happier that I kept growing until graduation."

"How tall are you?" Zeb asked.

"Six four. An inch taller than Luca."

"Dang, I'd need a ladder to kiss you," Zeb said.

"I'd punch your lights out before you got a foot on the first rung," Luca threatened.

Zeb chortled. "Will you please relax? There's no need to get all salty and shit."

Chyna smirked. "He's a bit territorial."

"I never would have guessed," Zeb deadpanned.

Luca didn't even bother denying it. "What's the deal with your ride?"

"Late as usual."

"Are you sure they're coming?" Luca asked.

"Yeah. I sent a text before I got off the bus," Zeb assured him. "Get going. I'm sure you guys can find something better to do than hang around here."

"You got that right," Luca agreed. "See you on Monday."

"Here at six?" Zeb asked.

"Yup."

Luca slung an arm around Chyna's waist, hefting his backpack on his right shoulder, and they headed toward 56th Street to catch the subway to the Upper West Side. Chyna's two- bedroom apartment was located on W 97th Street in a secure twelve-story building.

Although New York was supposed to be the great melting pot of cultures, and one of the most progressive cities when it came to LGBTQ rights—particularly in the fashion industry—it was hard to take anything for granted after the senseless massacre at the gay club in Orlando. Both sets of parents had urged Luca and Chyna to tone down the PDAs and be mindful of their surroundings at all times. In spite of the warnings, Luca found it difficult to let go of Chyna's hand despite a few dirty looks on the subway.

Being new to the city, and the subway system in particular, Luca was surprised how quickly they arrived at their destination. Following Chyna's lead, they blended into the exiting crowd and took the stairs up to the sidewalk.

"See that tall brick building?" Chyna pointed.

"Yeah."

"That's home."

"Let's go," Luca said, picking up his pace. The blue fob on Chyna's keychain unlocked the glass door of the apartment building, and he introduced Luca to Giorgi, the doorman on duty. He seemed friendly enough, but Luca wasn't in the mood to stand around and shoot the shit. He was desperate to get Chyna behind closed doors and do the things they'd talked about during their bouts of phone sex. The elevator door had barely shut when he swept Chyna into a bone-crushing hug.

"Luca, there's a camera in here."

Luca moaned and stepped back. "One of these days, I'm going to stop being so damn responsible and go off the rails."

"Warn me if that's about to happen."

Luca grinned. "Trust me, you'll be the first to know."

The elevator dinged the arrival at Chyna's floor, and they were sprinting down the hallway before the double doors swished shut. High on anticipation, Chyna fumbled with the keys.

"Open, open, open," Luca said in a teasing voice.

"Shut up," Chyna warned. "You're making me more nervous."

"God, I feel like I'm about to lose my mind," Luca said. "Hurry."

Once they were inside, Luca pinned Chyna against the door and kissed him hungrily. He'd been craving this—they both had—and finesse was forgotten in the heat of the moment. Teeth clacked and tongues clashed as they gorged on each other. As soon as they parted to come up for air, Luca toed off his shoes, pulled off his shirt, unbuttoned his jeans, and kicked them clear across the room after he extricated them from around his ankles. He kept his boxer briefs on, but they tented obscenely, and Chyna stared at his crotch longingly.

"Aren't you going to get undressed?" Luca asked before getting on his knees and looking up at the familiar face peering down at him.

Chyna removed the baseball hat, and his auburn hair fell forward in a silky curtain. Pale skin flushed in patches high above his cheekbones, and his lower lip quivered slightly.

"You do it," he urged in a strangled voice.

Luca's breath grew ragged as he fiddled with the zipper of Chyna's skinny jeans. When the fabric parted, he zeroed in on the head of Chyna's penis, which glistened above the waistband of his blue lace boy briefs. The smell of his arousal seeped through the flimsy fabric, making Luca light-headed. He leaned forward and licked the ooze from Chyna's slit, savoring the briny taste.

"Oh my God," Chyna breathed.

Hooking his fingers into the elastic, Luca tugged off the clothing in one efficient move, riveted on Chyna's cock as it lifted away from the tight confines and pointed at Luca enticingly.

"Fuuuuck…you're so ready for me."

He continued sliding the pants down Chyna's endless legs, and when they bunched at his ankles, Chyna helpfully stepped out of them. A wash of sunlight streamed through the open blinds, turning Chyna's skin golden as the rays bounced off the dusting of rose-gold hair he refused to shave or wax. The days of trying to look like a sleek female were gone, and Chyna preferred the natural look, especially after learning how much Luca adored the fuzz.

Luca rubbed his hands up and down Chyna's taut thighs and then drew him closer. Always on the lean side, Chyna's stomach was flat—almost concave—and his hip bones were more prominent than ever before. The trimmed hair above his swollen cock was a darker shade of auburn, and there was an intriguing cluster of freckles buried underneath the soft fur that Luca found endearing for some reason. Luca shut his eyes for a second, trying to get himself under control before he embarrassed them both and shot his load on the fake hardwood floor.

"Please," Chyna begged. "I'm a heartbeat away from coming."

Luca snorted. "This will be a record for both of us."

He cupped Chyna's balls with one hand and encircled his shaft with the other, sliding down the skin covering Chyna's glans and watching spellbound as the rosy head emerged, revealing another drop of clear liquid. The contrast between Chyna's uncut penis and his own circumcised organ was a constant source of fascination to both of them. Desperate noises were escaping from Chyna's throat as he got more and more excited.

"Luca," Chyna urged, "are you planning on looking all day or what?"

Goaded into action, Luca engulfed the rosy head. Spurts of warm cum flooded his mouth, and he swallowed convulsively, even as he busted into his boxers.

Chyna sank to his knees and ended up splayed on Luca who was on his back, spread out and boneless after the embarrassingly quick orgasm.

"Sheesh," Luca said, disgusted. "Eager much?"

Chyna giggled. "That was pitiful."

"I'll do better next time," Luca promised. "My intention is to remain naked for the next three days and show you what you've been missing."

"Sounds like an excellent plan," Chyna said. "Hungry?"

"I'm always hungry," Luca admitted. "Are you planning to cook, or will we be funding Domino's for the weekend?"

"I can make scrambled eggs," Chyna offered. "Anything fancier and we'll have to go out."

"Do you have bacon?"

"No."

"Bread?"

Nope."

"We're going grocery shopping later," Luca said.

"Okay. There's a deli close by," Chyna said. "They are open early and don't close until eleven o'clock."

"Let's go now," Luca said. "Stock up the fridge and hole up here for the duration."

"Don't you want to see the city?" Chyna asked. "Do some touristy things?"

"Not really," Luca said. "We can if you want, but I'd rather make love to you all weekend. Who knows when I'll get another opportunity to visit? Between football practice and studies, it'll be hard to get here."

"I'm surprised your coach let you off for three days."

"He wasn't happy, but I begged, and half the team is gone anyway."

"I'll visit you next time," Chyna said.

"That'll be great."

"Where would I stay since your dorm isn't an option?"

"We'll figure it out," Luca said. "There are several hotels in the area, or maybe Zeb can be persuaded to bunk in with someone else while you're in town."

"No, don't ask him. That wouldn't be fair."

"He won't mind. He's pretty cool."

"Does he have a girlfriend?"

"Not that I know of."

"He's straight, right?"

"Not sure."

"Well, if he starts groping you at night, make sure to kick him in the balls for me."

"Now who's being territorial?" Luca teased.

"Right? We're both selfish with each other."

"I don't care," Luca said. "You're mine, and sharing isn't part of my vocabulary."

Chapter Three

"YOU LOOK WELL-FUCKED and happy," Luca said softly, staring at Chyna's dreamy expression.

"I am," Chyna responded.

He combed through Chyna's tangles, shoving most of the hair away while hanging on to a few thick strands and twirling them around his forefinger. After spending most of the afternoon making up for the sexual drought they'd endured the last month, they were exhausted and hungry. It was almost seven o'clock in the evening, and their last meal was hours before. Luca swung his legs off the bed and was about to get up when Chyna grabbed his hand to stop him.

"Going somewhere?"

"I'd rather stay here," Luca admitted, "but you've got nothing to eat in this place—except for eggs, yogurt, and bananas—and if I don't get some dinner soon, I'll never be able to get it up again, let alone keep it up."

"Not my fault you finished all the junk food you bought earlier."

"I was starving, and all you have here is healthy crap."

"You can't subsist on chips, dip, and pizza forever," Chyna said.

"It's so much easier, though," Luca grumbled.

"Eventually it'll catch up to you."

"I guess," Luca admitted. "Where shall we go for dinner?"

"What are you in the mood for?"

"Italian?"

"Carb heavy," Chyna pointed out.

"So?"

"I'm trying to keep my daily count under a hundred grams and we had pizza earlier."

Luca frowned. "Are you on a diet?"

"No," Chyna said warily. "I'm trying to eat better."

"Why? You've never done it in the past," Luca stated.

"I can't afford to gain any weight."

"Says who?"

"Mel reminded me that most people in my line of work are underweight."

"When was this?"

"I was stuffing my face with a Big Mac the other day and she caught me midchew."

"Caught you? What the fuck," Luca said angrily. "Stop treating food like an illegal substance. You've always had a healthy appetite and eaten whatever the hell you wanted. You don't need to diet."

"What if things change?" Chyna asked. "They're talking about using me for male and female gigs. I can't compete with the likes of Kendall, Gigi, Kate, Bella, and Ymre if I gain weight."

"First of all, I don't know any of those people, so it's hard to picture your competition," Luca said. "And secondly, aren't they all women?"

"Yes, but—"

"Don't compare your body type and weight to girls," Luca said more gently. "You're a dude."

Chyna scowled. "I know what I am, Luca. Don't think I'm falling back into that black hole again, but weight issues in this industry are universal. Male models have to be rail thin, or they're ignored. Designers don't appreciate curves like other people. Anything that interferes with the way fabric is meant to drape or shape is undesirable. I'm new on the scene and want to make a good impression. That's why I'm being careful."

"I'm calling bullshit," Luca said, standing. "You haven't gained weight since I last saw you; in fact, you feel lighter. Don't make me regret this modeling decision before it's even taken off."

Chyna got on his knees and wrapped his arms around Luca's waist. He was still naked—they both were—and the steady look in the gorgeous blue eyes staring up at him went a long way to ease Luca's mind.

"I swear I'm not turning anorexic because I'm counting carbs," Chyna promised. "A lot of people do it, Luca. Not only models. I know you're only being protective, and I love and appreciate your concern, but you have nothing to worry about."

"Okay," Luca said, "but that doesn't lessen the shock of finding out you've turned into a health nut. You and I have always been on the same page when it comes to food. I hate not knowing what's going on with you."

"Come on," Chyna said reasonably. "We've talked about this separation endlessly. Don't spoil the weekend with unnecessary arguments over your fears of missing out."

"I'm sorry," Luca said, backing down. It took all his willpower to push away his concerns and be more sympathetic to Chyna's desire to eat healthy. If he were honest, he'd admit he hadn't had a balanced meal since living home. Subsisting on pizza and burgers alone couldn't be good for his body.

"Are we okay?" Chyna asked. His hands had dropped down to Luca's butt cheeks and were massaging him lightly.

Luca pressed his rising cock against Chyna and joked, "Any better and we'll have to order takeout."

Chyna slapped him playfully. "Get in the shower and we'll continue this after dinner."

Luca mock saluted and left the bedroom. For the amount of money Chyna was paying for the apartment, he'd expected more than one bathroom but was informed that anything additional would have jacked up the rent considerably. At least it was large and ultramodern. The future architect in him was already picking apart the layout and choice of fixtures. He stepped into the glass-enclosed shower stall and turned on the hot water. The pressure was good and there was plenty of room for a tall man to navigate without knocking his elbows against the sides. Definitely a plus.

While shampooing, Luca considered Chyna's mild rebuke about his fear of missing out. Was it the real issue, or was he worried that, once again, Chyna was teetering on the dangerous line of gender dysphoria, which had made his early years a living hell. Chyna had struggled throughout high school to get comfortable with his undeniably male body. Luca had been by his side during the process, and he'd vowed to support Chyna's ultimate decision, no matter which gender he chose to identify with, but it had taken a toll on Luca as well. One he rarely talked about. He didn't want his personal preferences to influence Chyna in any way. Dr. Jody Williams, one of Chyna's foster fathers, and Dr. Sean Andrews, the endocrinologist who'd helped Chyna through his painful metamorphosis, applauded Luca for his unwavering support and Swiss-like ability to stay neutral.

Nonetheless, if pressed, Luca would have admitted he hoped Chyna would get comfortable as a guy because Luca was definitely gay, and not bisexual as he'd once thought.

Looking back, he remembered the confusion he dealt with the summer before high school started. He'd been wrestling with feelings for Chip, while also noticing Chyna, who was passing for female at the time. It had caused a lot of anxiety on multiple fronts but was resolved in the end when the lies were exposed.

Bottom line, Luca loved everything about Chyna's male form, although conversely, found the occasional cross-dressing in private a guilty pleasure. Finding lace panties after peeling off Chyna's blue jeans was a huge turn-on. Initially, Luca was convinced he'd need psychiatric help as well, but when he spoke to his dad about his fondness for feminine undergarments, he was told in no uncertain terms that it was okay. There were no hard and fast rules when it came to sexual kinks, and thank God his father and stepfather were the coolest guys on the planet. It made him wonder if one or both of them had the same lingerie fetish, but he hadn't worked up the courage to ask. And ultimately, a negative or positive reply wouldn't change anything. He liked what he liked.

When Chyna made his decision to abandon all thoughts of transitioning to female, Luca was relieved and finally shared his feelings on the subject. He'd held Chyna who'd cried in his arms, begging Luca to be patient with him as he slowly shed the girl he'd been living as for years. It had been a joint collaboration on their part, and the young man Luca was hopelessly in love with had slowly crystallized into a stronger and much more interesting individual—a perfect combination of masculine and feminine traits Luca found alluring and irresistible.

The one residual that had stubbornly clung to Chyna throughout high school had been his desire to model. Despite Luca's fears, and the advice from Chyna's foster fathers and other medical professionals, Chyna insisted that this detour into the fleeting and oftentimes catty world of modeling was something he needed to explore. For years, he'd thought of nothing else, and Melinda had encouraged him. This way, Chyna informed Luca, he'd learn firsthand if modeling was the right career choice or merely a carryover from childhood. Chyna swore he was confident enough to withstand any amount of peer pressure prevalent among members of the fashion industry.

But that was back then. Already, Chyna's diet was being restructured. What would come next? A growing sense of dread that something awful was about to happen had settled into a hollow pit in Luca's gut. He wasn't sure if it was a premonition or basic paranoia, but he needed to shrug it off before things between them turned ugly. Normally compliant when it came to Luca's wishes, Chyna would draw a line in the sand if Luca got bossy and insisted on doing things his way. They'd never had that kind of dynamic, and now wasn't a good time to start. Not when they were both embarking on new lives far away from the safety of their Barrington, Illinois, suburb. It was essential to keep the lines of communication open, so he could be there for Chyna if the need arose.

During the course of their dinner, at a small Italian bistro, Luca recounted his first two weeks at Cornell, starting with his impressions of his roommate.

"He seems pretty laid-back," Chyna said.

"A bit spoiled, but I can deal with it."

"In what way?" Chyna asked.

"Zeb forgets he's not in the Philippines anymore and acts totally surprised when I remind him to pick up his shit. Dude doesn't even know how to fold his clothes."

Chyna laughed. "Seriously?"

"Yeah," Luca said. "My maternal grandparents were raised over there. Wealthy people have servants to do most of their daily chores, which is great, except when you leave the country and can't figure out how to survive in the real world. Zeb didn't know to separate his laundry or what kind of soap to buy, much less how to run the machine. Dude, it was lame but so damned funny I was cracking up."

"So...you've been helping him out?"

"Without doing his work."

"You'll make a good dad someday," Chyna said wistfully.

"Chyna...."

"Just saying."

Luca didn't want to have this conversation again. They'd had it the night of the senior prom, and it had put a damper on an otherwise perfect moment. If Chyna hadn't been born intersex, it wouldn't be up for discussion. The conversation might have veered off toward adoption or surrogacy, but since Chyna had a couple of female reproductive organs, the idea of having Luca's baby had taken root, and, regretfully, he'd had to burst the beautiful bubble with the harsh facts.

"I still have a uterus," Chyna reminded him.

"But no vagina or ovaries," Luca pointed out. "It's scientifically impossible for us to create a child."

"Maybe science will improve by the time we're ready to start a family."

"Have you talked to anyone about this?" Luca asked, feeling a little shell-shocked.

"No."

"So you don't really know if it's possible or not."

"Why are you tripping, Luca?"

"Um, maybe because you've opened up a whole new can of worms."

Chyna laughed. "Breathe, babe. This scenario is so far down the road I can't even see it."

Luca scrubbed his face with both hands. "Then why'd you bring it up?"

"I'm weird like that."

"Jeez...I'll have to agree with you this time."

"How's your lasagna?" Chyna asked, deftly changing the subject.

"It's great. What about your hold-the-noodles-and-rice veal scaloppini?"

Chyna smiled. "Delicious and I don't miss the carbs."

"Okay," Luca said with an exasperated eye roll. "Moving away from food. Tell me about that prick, Ian."

"Talk about ruining a fun dinner."

"That bad?"

"He's the Tom Brady of photogs and acts like it," Chyna said.

"Has he tried hitting on you?"

Chyna cocked his head. "Not yet. Why? Are you jealous?"

"Do I have reason to be?"

"Absolutely not," Chyna assured him.

"Then I won't bring it up again."

"Thank you," Chyna said. "Anyone on campus caught your eye?"

"Worried much?" Luca asked, smiling.

"Do I have reason to be?" Chyna echoed his own words.

"Fuck, no."

"Then we're golden." Chyna smiled. "Are your body fluids sufficiently replenished?"

"I thought I'd have some dessert. Want to split a chocolate sundae?"

"Sure," Chyna said. "There's a reason I didn't have carbs with dinner. I'm saving my calories for the bad stuff."

"You're seriously disturbed," Luca commented.

"That's why you love me," Chyna said, reaching for Luca's hand across the table. "I keep it interesting."

"I do love you," Luca said.

"Madly?"

"Yes," Luca said. "Even when you're confusing as hell."

Chapter Four

ON SUNDAY AFTERNOON, Luca sat in on my interview with potential roommate, Sarah Mitchell, a rangy brunette calling herself Xara. She was an LA transplant who'd been modeling a little longer than me. We'd had a preliminary conversation over the phone a few days before, and I was prepared to offer her the room until we shared a pizza. Xara disappeared after she'd inhaled two slices and Luca followed shortly after. When he returned, he was frowning.

"Something wrong?"

"She's a no," he whispered. "I found her hugging the porcelain goddess. She's obviously got body image issues, and you don't need to be saddled with that kind of shit."

"Are you sure? What if it's food poisoning?"

"Do you feel sick?"

"No," I admitted, "but I hate to dismiss her over one incident."

"Do you want to deal with a bulimic on a daily basis?"

Uncertain, I suggested, "What if I came right out and asked? Isn't that better than assuming the worse?"

Luca didn't get a chance to answer my question before Xara returned.

"So what do you think?" she asked. "Can I start moving my stuff?"

I hesitated, reluctant to make an enemy so early in my career, but at the same time, I was inclined to follow Luca's lead. He'd always been better than me when it came to first impressions. He must have sensed my conflict, and reached for my hand, squeezing it gently.

"Didn't you say you had a couple more interviews scheduled for today?"

Grabbing Luca's lifeline, I nodded and turned to Xara. "Can I let you know tomorrow?"

"I may not be interested tomorrow," she said stiffly.

"I'll have to take my chances."

Xara's gaze flicked between Luca and me, her eyes narrowing.

"You'd better grow some balls if you want to make it in this town. Last time we talked, this was a done deal," she accused. "I guess your boyfriend doesn't like me for whatever reason."

"That's not it," I lied. "Deciding on a roommate without meeting in person is risky. I told you that over the phone. There were no guarantees on my end."

"FYI," Xara said as a parting shot, "I'm not some kind of lowlife." She picked up her purse and slammed the door on her way out.

"Now I feel like the world's biggest loser."

"Don't," Luca said. "She puked before she even digested her pizza. Pretty sure you'd rather not deal with that on the daily."

"How would it become my problem, though? She's not going to expect me to clean up her mess."

"You don't know that," Luca said. "There's only one bathroom, and I can't imagine you'll want to use it after someone's hurled. Plus, she may end up becoming a friend, and you'll get dragged into her drama. Is that how you envision the next year?"

"Not really."

"Then trust me, Chyna. You can do better than her."

"I'm not exactly low maintenance," I reminded him.

"Maybe, but the way I see it, this is your apartment, so you can afford to be picky. You'll have plenty of challenges trying to learn a new business, and it would be helpful to have a roommate who doesn't add to your stress."

"Do you think I'm better off with someone who isn't in the modeling industry?"

Luca shrugged. "Honestly, I don't know. Why don't we wait and see who shows up next?"

"Okay."

The next person to apply was a guy who looked like he'd walked off the pages of an Abercrombie & Fitch catalog. He was seriously hot, and I could feel the shift in Luca's body language the minute he set eyes on the blond. In the four years we'd been together, I'd never given anyone a second glance, so Luca had no reason to fear the presence of another attractive male, but this current setup was turning him into a twitchy Rottweiler.

"What's wrong with Aaron?"

"I don't like him," Luca said stubbornly.

"You don't even know him," I exclaimed as we huddled in the bedroom for a private consultation.

"Dude, he looks reckless."

"Luca, get real."

"I'm going with my gut instinct and Aaron's a no."

Tackling him onto the bed, I lay on his chest and pressed my forehead against his. "There's no need to be jealous."

"It's not that," Luca admitted sheepishly. "There's something about him that feels wrong."

Patiently, I attempted to ease his mind. "I'll be surrounded by the world's hottest models all day. It's unavoidable, babe, but when you work in a candy store long enough, you become immune to the product. Stop assuming I'm incapable of resisting the first stud who looks my way."

"I know," Luca conceded, "but you're in a new environment, and you've got to admit, New York and the modeling industry are far more exciting than Barrington High School. I can't help worrying and wondering who's going to be available when you're lonely and need some sort of TLC. I'm too far to get here in time to do damage control."

"Is that what you think? I'm going to be spiraling out of control on the daily and reaching for my roommate?"

Feeling my outrage, Luca reasoned, "I've been watching your blind side for years, and the idea of being too far away to be effective is making me crazy."

"No shit."

I moved away as my temper spiked. Assuming I'd fall into a stranger's arms because he wasn't around was seriously pissing me off. He tried pulling me back, but I twisted away.

"Shut it down, Luca. Stop treating me like a sex addict who'll jump into bed with the first available body."

"It's not you," he said lamely. "It's the other guys I don't trust."

"Same difference," I ranted. "If I was that weak, I'd be on my knees all day long. News flash, boyfriend. I have mastered the fine art of telling people to fuck off."

Luca pounced on my statement. "Who hit on you?"

"What the hell! I'm bringing it up to prove a point. You have to trust me, or this separation will never work."

I left the bedroom to give Aaron the bad news.

When I returned, Luca was still lying on my bed with one arm crossed over his eyes. Sounding more like a surly child than the man I loved, he asked, "Do you want me to pack up and go?"

"No," I argued, "but I'd like you to stop acting like you're fourteen."

Luca sat up and swung his legs off the bed. "I don't know what's wrong with me," he admitted. "I've never been this insecure in my life."

Touched by his admission, I sank to my knees in front of him and looked into his eyes. They were troubled and glittered with suppressed tears. The Luca I'd known had always been confident and easygoing. This new version of him was unattractive and, if I was being honest, a bit hateful. I knew we'd be in trouble if something didn't change. He bit his lower lip, which had begun to quiver.

"Babe," I suggested carefully, "maybe you should call Chip. You know he's the best at talking people off a ledge. I can't tell you how many times he's done it for me."

"Good idea," he said softly.

My twin was Luca's best friend as well as my champion and confidant. He was super smart, pragmatic, and knew me as well, if not better, than anyone else. He'd tell Luca to stop overthinking our geographical challenges. Hooking up with others, no matter what the provocation, wasn't the way either of us rolled. Luca needed the reassurance, however, and I couldn't think of anyone better suited than Chip. It would be beneficial for both of us if they kept in touch. Luca had used him as a sounding board through four years of high school, in addition to three years of middle school. Why should it stop now?

I left the room when Luca reached for his phone, wanting to give him the privacy he deserved. Later, he found me huddled on the sofa, browsing channels on the flat-screen. Silently, Luca waited to see if I settled on anything specific but must have realized the mindless surfing was my way of avoiding another argument. He grabbed my feet and began kneading them gently.

"I'll need more than a foot rub to put me in a better mood."

"I was hoping it might be a good start," Luca confessed.

"Things will go back to normal once you stop acting like my bodyguard."

Luca slumped against the backrest and closed his eyes. "I'm sorry."

I moved to straddle him. "Look at me."

His eyelids fluttered open. Despite the anguish on his face, he was still gorgeous. How could he think I'd be interested in anyone else when I had him?

"Please don't be upset," I said softly. "It sucks that we're living so far apart right now and things are radically different for both of us, but we knew this was going to be difficult when we planned our future. I'll be facing people and circumstances I've never dealt with before, and so will you. We can't lose sight of our goals because things aren't ideal at the moment. I need my confident guy to keep it together, or I'll flounder, and what good will that do? I'll be miserable if I fail and you'll bear the brunt of it."

"All good points except you're alone in this big city. Melinda's going back to Chicago soon, and that'll leave you with zero support. Choosing the right roommate, someone who'll watch your back without being a threat to our relationship, is important to me. Am I making sense?"

Clearly, jealousy was still plaguing him. "I'm aware you have this compelling need to protect me, and I'll admit it's a little scary out there, but we've always trusted each other. Things don't have to change because we're apart. And for the record, I would never cheat on you. On the off chance I'm ever tempted, and I'm throwing this out as a hypothetical, I'd discuss it with you first. I'm hoping you'd do the same on your end."

Luca drew me down and wrapped me in a warm embrace. "Cheating never occurred to me when we talked about our future, but now that we've started the first phase of our careers, I'm fixating on all the things that might pull us apart instead of relying on our love to keep us together. Just talking about the possibility of anyone laying a hand on you makes me want to punch a hole in the wall."

"I won't put myself into that kind of situation."

"You can't predict the future," Luca reasoned.

"Maybe not," I agreed. "But you and I were meant to be together. I knew it back in the day when I was wearing a bra stuffed with tissues, and after all we've been through to get here, I'm more confident than ever. Let's make a pact to focus on the positive, okay? We're a phone call away and we'll always have the weekends."

"Not if you have a photo shoot or I have a game. We can't count on that to happen like clockwork."

"We'll have to be flexible and adjust as needed."

"I guess," Luca grumbled. "So, do you want to call Aaron back and ask him to move in?"

"You prefer him over Xara?"

"Who would you be more comfortable with?" Luca asked. "I think they're both lousy choices."

I hesitated. "Actually, there's one more person we haven't met. He's also with Elite and Mel thinks we might be a good fit."

"What makes you think this one will be different?"

"He's a trans guy so maybe he'd be more sympathetic to my old issues?"

"You don't have issues," Luca said adamantly.

"There's the cross-dressing," I reminded him. "A regular dude might balk if he sees me in pink panties."

"Why in fuck would you let that happen?"

His tone set me off again, and I got right in his face and fucking snarled. "Shut it! There's only one bathroom in this fricking apartment! I might forget something and have to go back and forth in my underwear."

Luca's eyes widened.

"Oh my God, will you stop imagining the worse?"

"Sorry," Luca apologized. "I suck at this new normal."

"That's becoming more obvious by the minute. If it's any consolation, Mel had nothing but nice things to say about this guy. I didn't give him an appointment because I thought Xara had the spot."

"What's his name?"

"Alex something."

"That's not helpful," Luca complained. "Do you have his number?"

"Yeah, Mel texted it last week."

"See if he'd be willing to come over today."

I reached for my phone and began scrolling through my texts until I located the number. After three rings, a sleepy voice answered.

"Hello?"

"Is this Alex?"

"Uh-huh. Who are you?"

"Chyna Davidson. Melinda Watson from Elite gave me your number. Are you still looking for an apartment?"

"I sure am."

"Do you have time to come over today and check out my place?"

"Where?"

I gave him the address, and Alex agreed to swing by an hour later. After disconnecting, I slumped on Luca's chest and took a huge breath. "I hope he works out."

"Me too," Luca agreed.

"Crossing fingers."

When the downstairs entry buzzer rang, Luca and I were still cuddling on the sofa watching a rerun of *The Big Bang Theory*. Grabbing my phone, which had an app that allowed me to unlock the main entrance, I confirmed it was Alex Boulet and let him in.

We waited at the front door when a stunning biracial man stepped out of the elevator. He was taller than me, which meant he was at least six foot five inches, and he had a Burberry dog carrier slung on his right arm. The furry black face staring at us was adorable. I squealed in delight.

Alex's facial expression was a combination of pride and panic. "Sorry I didn't mention I have a pet. Is it okay, sugar?"

"Oh my God, yes," I assured him. Luca and I were both animal lovers, and I didn't even realize I wanted one until I saw my prospective roommate. "I'm not sure what the rules are with regards to our landlord, but we'll work it out. You'll have to pay any additional fees involved."

"Absolutely," Alex said. "Bacon is four years old, neutered, and crate trained. He won't be any trouble at all."

"Bacon?" I stared at the itty-bitty dog, bemused.

"It's like this," Alex said in a melodic tone that was soothing as well as pleasant. "I wanted a pot-bellied pig, and my parents got me a poodle instead. They said he'd be a better fit."

I couldn't help smiling. "In what sense would he be better?"

"Sugar, take a good look. Can you imagine a genderqueer teen walking down the streets of Baton Rouge with a pig? At the time, I didn't have enough confidence to pull it off, and my father was convinced I was asking for trouble by drawing more attention to my gangly self. I cried for days. Ugly, fat tears that made me look positively hideous. Finally, they came home with this sweet thing, but I named him Bacon in protest. It took several days for me to realize they were right and I was dead wrong. By the time I fell in love with my little darling, he was answering to Bacon so it stuck."

"May I hold him?"

Alex handed over the fluffy bundle, who wriggled and licked his way straight to my heart. Luca was beside me in a minute, adding his praise and trying to pry Bacon away. I passed him over so I could concentrate on Alex.

He appeared to be a little older than us, but not by much. He mentioned his Creole heritage in passing, which explained the accent, striking green eyes, and light skin. He was dressed in black with a red scarf providing the only color.

"Dang, you're imposing," I muttered. "It's a good thing we're polar opposites, or I'd never stand a chance in this business."

Alex waved away my concerns with a flick of his wrist. "Aww, sugar, don't sell yourself short. Gingers are all the rage these days."

"Thanks." The endearment was sweet and made me more comfortable for some reason. It seemed like I'd known Alex for ages instead of fifteen minutes. "Would you like to see the apartment?"

"I'd love to."

After the brief tour, Luca and I talked in private for a few minutes.

"What do you think?" I asked.

"He seems nice and Bacon is a plus."

"Right? I like him. Are you getting any of your weird vibes?"

"Zip."

"Then it's a go."

"How soon can you move in?" I asked Alex when we walked out of the bedroom.

"What about tomorrow?"

"That's great," Luca said. "Is there anything we can do to make this easy for you?"

"Nah, I've got this. But thank you for asking," Alex added.

"You're welcome," Luca replied.

"Please don't come before eleven," I interjected.

Alex looked up at the ceiling in mock horror. "I wouldn't dream of it."

Chapter Five

WE HAD CHINESE takeout for dinner that night while binge-watching *Mr. Robot*, a show Luca enjoyed but I found bewilderingly depressing. After ten minutes, I decided to make better use of my time by washing and blow-drying my hair.

Luca's behavior continued to baffle me. One minute, he was savagely territorial and, just as suddenly, oblivious to my movements. So engrossed in his show, I could have disappeared in a puff of smoke and he wouldn't have noticed until dinnertime. After bickering for the last few hours, I thought makeup sex was in order, but he didn't seem interested.

After my shower, I gathered up my damp hair into a messy knot on top of my head and walked out in nothing but purple lace boy briefs. Luca didn't even glance my way. Frustrated, I retreated to the bathroom, put on some dark-gray eye shadow, a touch of pink blush, and a dab of lip gloss. After that, I blew my hair dry, spritzed, finger combed, and positioned the waves artfully around my face. The last time I felt this glamorous had been four months ago, the night of our senior prom. Melinda had come over to help me dress, and I waited apprehensively as she studied me from head to toe.

"Well?" I asked hopefully. "Will Luca take one look at me and think he's the luckiest guy on earth or get back in the limousine and head in the opposite direction?"

Notorious for her forthright manner, she inspected me like I was about to step onto a Milan runway. "The gray eye shadow works well."

I beamed. "I thought it would be more dramatic than brown."

"You thought right," Melinda agreed. "The blue eyeliner and mascara are a bit over the top, but you've carried it off with your usual style."

"Thanks." I exhaled with relief. So far, I was two for two, which was always a good thing when it came to Melinda. She'd been a makeup artist for years and kept up with constantly changing trends.

Continuing her evaluation, Melinda tracked down my face. "Barely there blush. Perfect."

I grinned and gave her a thumbs-up.

"Your lipstick should be a shade darker," Melinda suggested. Before I could protest, Melinda raised her right hand to stop me. "I know Luca doesn't like the feel or taste, but he's not going to be kissing you until much later."

"Yes, but—"

"But nothing," Melinda said. "You'll show up at the prom looking your best. I don't care what happens afterward."

I rolled my eyes. "Fine."

Melinda stepped forward and dabbed more gloss on my lips with the spongy wand.

"That's better," she said, taking a back step. "With your smoky eyes and pale skin, you could pass for a bloodsucker. Why not add to the illusion with a spot of Merlot on those luscious lips."

"Wow, thanks for that visual."

"Vamps are hot, girlfriend. Let's talk about your hair," Melinda said.

"What about it?"

"It should go up."

"No, Luca likes it down."

"Chyna, a man bun is a lot more fashionable. You've been sporting that tired old look for too long. It's time to refresh your image now that you're embarking on a new career."

"Nuh-uh. I'm proud of my hair and like to show it off."

"Your hair is undoubtedly one of your finest features, but you're not modeling for Pantene products tonight," Melinda reminded me. "Your classmates are expecting another disaster, and we're going to prove them wrong."

"Why do you think I haven't been to a dance since freshman year?"

"Since you've decided to show up, let's make Luca proud."

"There's nothing I want more," I agreed.

"Trust me on the hair."

"But a man bun?"

"It'll look better with your tux," Melinda explained patiently.

"All right."

I sank down on my bed, stretching my legs in front of me. Shoeless at the moment, I admired my painted toes and waited patiently while

Melinda brushed and gathered the strands into a trendy knot on top of my head. Bobbie pins dug into my scalp as she anchored the hair into place.

"Ow."

"Don't be such a man," Melinda admonished.

I mock laughed. "Don't girls feel any pain?"

"Of course, but we're a lot more stoic."

"And if one happens to have bits and pieces of both?"

"Then you take the best of both sexes and roll them into one fabulous Chyna."

"Luca will probably pull the pins out before the night is over."

"Hon, you can get naked for all I care. Right now, I'm focusing on the grand entrance."

Did she know the plan? How could she when I'd purposely kept it to myself. Luca had accused me of oversharing with her, and I swore it would be different this time. Mel had been the first adult who'd stripped away my mask and given me the confidence I needed to stop pretending to be the daughter my mother wished she'd had. The alternative, embracing the anatomy I'd been born with, was terrifying. Mel was a transgender woman and had enough experience to look beyond the obvious. Her sympathetic ear and ongoing support had made her indispensable in my life. Luca didn't understand the ties that bound us so tightly, especially when I shared info regarding our sex life. That was off limits, he'd warned.

Tonight was the night we were going to take the next step. Throughout high school, Luca had been sensitive to my state of mind and never pressed for more than I was willing to give. When I broached the subject a few weeks ago, hinting at the possibility of spending prom night together, and celebrating the end of one era and the beginning of another with unrestricted lovemaking, Luca jumped on the idea. Normally, Mel would have had all the salacious details by now, but I honored Luca's request for privacy.

When she was done, I thanked her and kissed her on the cheek.

"Aww...my pleasure, hon. Have a wonderful time. Let's hope you wipe out every single bad memory and bank several new ones that will make you smile instead of cry."

"I'll do my best."

Melinda grabbed her purse and, giving me one last hug, walked out of the room.

I took one more look in the mirror and smiled at my reflection. Melinda had been right. The man bun was an inspired touch as was the gray chemise with the lace border. They added a racier element to the ultraconservative tuxedo, turning me into the uber-stud Luca deserved.

Three years prior, I'd stood in front of a full-length mirror in a similar room, wearing a brown strapless gown and wristlet. My hair had spilled down my shoulders like a russet and gold pashmina shawl. Back then, my biggest problem had been hiding my penis from Luca. Having recently uncovered my mother's twisted scheme to manipulate our medical records, so school authorities wouldn't realize she'd been passing me off as a girl for years, I was barely talking to her. Even her lame attempts to compliment my attire fell on deaf ears. If I had known it would be the last time I laid eyes on her, I might have been more forgiving. But that was then, and tonight things would be different. I prayed for a much better ending this time around.

Luca's appreciative smile and ruddy cheeks signaled his approval.

All eyes were on us when we walked into the gym, and this time things went according to plan. There were no dramatic Stephen King "Carrie" moments when we were crowned Prom King and Partner. We'd danced nonstop, and when it was time to get back in the limo and head to Luca's house for the after-prom party, we'd held hands quietly, anticipating the moment when we'd be able to slip away. Having the party at his home had made the logistics a lot easier.

It was almost three in the morning by the time we were able to meet in Luca's room. Silently, and by mutual agreement, we didn't turn on the lights. There was a full moon that night, and silver beams snuck in through the partially closed slats of the blinds, giving us all the illumination we needed. We'd kissed and groped through four years of high school and had seen each other's most pertinent body parts in fits and starts, usually in someone's car, or a stolen moment pressed up against the door of a closet or restroom. This was the first time we'd be completely nude and free to explore without interruptions.

Predictably, Luca's first thought was to unpin my hair. Clips dropped to the floor as he pulled them out one by one. When the heavy strands fell through his fingers, he sighed in appreciation and the kissing grew more intense. Blood pounded in my ears when I felt Luca's naked body pressing me down on the mattress. His skin was as smooth as silk, and his hard cock butting up against mine felt incredible.

Since this was our first time, we decided against a condom. When Luca finally breached me after endless foreplay, which included finger fucking, I waited for the fireworks and toe-curling pleasure, but nothing happened. It felt a little weird. Then Luca moved, slowly thrusting in and out, changing angles in tiny increments until he found the magic spot that sent a zap of pleasure I'd never experienced before. It made me arch my back and grip his biceps. Luca swallowed my moans with deep kisses, and after that, it turned into a passionate blur of grinding and twisting heat that exploded into tiny fragments of pure bliss.

Cuddling after sex took on a whole new meaning when we were still naked and body fluids trickled out of an unfamiliar place. Luca twirled strands of my hair round and round his forefinger before he broke the silence.

"Did you know I was conceived on a night like this?"

"No," I replied. "You never told me this story."

"My parents had drunk sex after their senior prom, and I showed up nine months later. It's a bit demoralizing to know they had me with hardly any effort whereas you and I would have to jump through some major hoops to have a kid. And I love you way more than Dad ever loved Mom."

"I love you too," I said softly. "But even with medical intervention, it would never work. You're getting a factory defect, babe."

"No, I'm not," Luca said fiercely. "I love you as you are. I'm not sure why I even bothered mentioning babies. All I want is you by my side for the rest of our lives."

Luca knocked on the bathroom door, wrenching me out of the past and squarely back into the present.

"What's taking so long?" he asked when I opened the door.

"Sorry, I got sidetracked."

"By what?"

"My hair."

"It looks nice, but I have to piss."

"Go for it," I said, leaving him and heading toward my room. My last photo shoot had been for a line of women's clothing, and the designer, who'd insisted on being present, had fallen in love with my androgynous look. At the end, she'd handed over a shirt, telling me to take the gift as a memento of our first collaboration. I gratefully accepted the deep-green silk top with a high neck and modernized hanging sleeves. The color suited my complexion, and the flashes of skin glimpsed through the slits in the sleeves were at once sexy and romantic.

In the living room, Luca was back on the sofa, engrossed in his show. I struck a dramatic pose and cleared my throat to get his attention. He turned toward me and gawked. "Whoa! You look like you stepped out of a fashion magazine."

Preening, I struck another pose. "You like?"

"Hell, yeah." Luca was at my side in seconds. "You're hot as fuck."

"Let's go downtown."

"It's ten o'clock at night," Luca protested.

"Who cares? We're in a city that never sleeps," I reminded him. "Neither of us has to be up early tomorrow. Let's play tourist for a few hours."

"I'd rather stay here and make love."

I cupped his package and squeezed playfully. "Anticipation will make it that much better."

Luca shook his head. "Can we at least take the edge off before we go out?"

I stepped out of reach. "Not so fast."

"Aww...come on."

"Nope. It took me an hour to get ready, and I don't want you ruining my hard work. Go and put on your shoes and jacket."

"You're a tease."

"I'm determined and resolute. You, on the other hand, are ruled by your cock."

Luca sneered. "You're as much a man as me."

"But I trained on the other team for years," I reminded him. "My lust is firmly under control."

"Lift your shirt so I can check out your package."

"Are you challenging me?"

Luca waggled his eyebrows. "I get to blow you if you're hard."

I knew I'd win this round because I'd tucked to accommodate my skinny jeans. I didn't want an unsightly bulge to ruin my look.

"Deal."

I lifted my shirt and Luca frowned. "You're a better man than me," he said begrudgingly.

"Told you," I said, winking at him. Hell, I'd had years of practice willing my erection to behave.

After Luca was ready to go, we took the subway to 33rd Street and walked to 350 Fifth Avenue, where the Empire State Building was located. Once we were out and about, Luca stopped mentioning his mild case of blue balls and got into the tourist mindset. We were in plenty of time before the two o'clock closing, and the line wasn't as bad as I'd anticipated.

It hadn't been possible to see all the New York City attractions when I was apartment hunting with Clark and Jody. This spontaneous suggestion was a welcome addition to our Labor Day weekend, and the photos we took a pleasant reminder. It was a clear night, and the city, with its bright lights, lay sprawled out before us like a glittering postcard. I soaked up the sight of Manhattan, the center of the beauty and fashion industry, a world I hoped to conquer. The journey I'd traveled from mixed-up kid to aspiring model had been successful thanks in large part to Luca. His love had been the unwavering constant in my life, and I felt compelled to mark the visit to this iconic landmark with an affirmation of sorts.

Turning away from the breathtaking view, I faced Luca. "Thank you for bringing me here tonight. We've shared so many beginnings, and seeing this together for the first time makes it extra special."

"You know I'd do anything for you."

I moved closer.

Sensing a shift in mood, Luca asked, "Why so serious?"

I hugged him around the waist tightly. "It's hard to find the right words to tell you how much you mean to me."

"Just say you love me," Luca said. In a teasing tone, he added, "If you want to throw in a memorable mile-high blow job, that'll be fantastic."

"It only applies to airplanes."

"Maybe," Luca fudged. "If you check the building stats on the plaque by the elevator, you'll see it's high enough to qualify for the special club."

"That's all well and good, my well-informed future architect, but I'm not getting arrested for indecent behavior."

"Chicken?"

"Aren't you worried you'll end up in jail?"

"Maybe a little," Luca admitted. "I'm willing to wait until we're home."

"Thank God." I exhaled with relief. "I'd do anything for you, but the BJ would have been mediocre at best. It's hard to concentrate when you're thinking of cops."

"But you were willing and that says a lot."

We kissed and, when we parted, stayed in each other's arms taking in the sights.

"I have a confession to make," Luca said softly against my ear. "Loving you is the easy part. It's the letting go that needs work."

"I know you've had your doubts about this modeling gig, but you've never asked me to quit, which is huge. I think the control thing will fade in time."

"I hope so. You deserve to be happy," Luca said. "Even if it takes you away from me for days on end. It might take a while, but I think I can do the right thing. Promise you'll never let distance come between us."

"Promise," I said. "We'll Skype or text as often as we can."

"Do you think you'll still be modeling by this time next year?"

"To be honest, I have no idea if I'll make it past this month."

"Why would you say something so negative?" Luca asked. "I thought that last photographer loved you."

"We got off to a rocky start, and I'm not sure if he'll ask for me again. Ian has beautiful people at his beck and call. It's hard to remain at the top of the list when you're being nudged aside by a fresh face. I'm too new and can't predict how well I'll do in the long run. What if they get tired of boys who look like girls and vice versa? People can be shallow when it comes to beauty trends. Ten years ago, having a big ass was a definite no-no. Now, people are actually getting implants to augment ass cheeks. It's insane."

"Your ass is perfect."

"You're biased."

"Chyna," Luca said. "I've been obsessed with you since I was fifteen."

"I know," I said. "And I was crushing on you long before then."

"Which only proves we're meant to be together," Luca said with certainty.

"I'm terrified of failing," I admitted in a shaky voice. "I don't have any special skills to fall back on. The only thing I've got going in my favor is beauty and that fades. What if you decide you want a family after all? What do we do then?"

Luca shook me by the shoulders gently. "Hey, slow down. Take a deep breath and think about it. You're nineteen, decades away from retirement. And why are you having a meltdown over children all of a sudden? Is this the old Chyna talking? If so, would you please ask her to go away? There's no room in our relationship for a three-way."

I burst out laughing. "Thanks for the reality check."

Luca joined in, but when the laughter faded, he asked, "What's going through that gorgeous head of yours? Are you having second thoughts about anything? Talk to me."

"I'm not sure," I admitted. "Maybe I'm starting to realize this career path I've chosen is risky as hell."

"You're going to be a fantastic model. When you get tired of doing this, you'll join me at Cornell and become an interior designer like we planned."

"What makes you think I'll stand apart from the horde of hopefuls who show up every day?"

"Because you're determined and resolute," Luca said, echoing my earlier statement.

"That's with you and Chip around to boost my ego and reassure me when I'm doubting myself. I have no clue how I'll make it without you two."

"You'll be fine."

We left the observatory shortly after and decided to walk instead of taking the subway uptown. Since the weather was cooperating and our feet weren't protesting, we took our time, turning left on 42nd Street, heading toward Times Square. We walked hand in hand, stopping occasionally to glance into a shop window, enjoying the energetic vibe of a city teeming with life. Growling stomachs and the enticing smell of sizzling garlic, sausage, and cheese lured us into a pizza joint.

I noticed the look of relief on Luca's face when I reached for a second greasy slice. Had he honestly been worrying about an eating disorder? God, the poor guy had enough on his plate without adding one more thing to his long list of potential problems.

Eventually we got tired and decided to head home. It was close to two in the morning when we rounded the corner and spied the familiar brick building. Before I reached for my key fob to open the front door, I thought I heard someone call my name. Incredulously, I turned around, looking left and right. There was nothing.

"Did you hear that?" I asked Luca.

Frowning, Luca nodded. "Yeah. What in the fuck?"

We searched the street and the surrounding buildings. Far off in the distance, someone was pushing an old grocery cart piled high with soda cans and bottles. The person stopped to pick up another discarded beer bottle lying on the street. The glass clinked when it landed on top of the pile.

I wasn't sure if I'd imagined the voice, but since Luca had also heard the same thing, I decided it was the wind playing tricks on our imagination.

Luca took the fob out of my hand and waved it at the electronic pad to unlock the door.

"Let's go," he said. "I think we're both tired and hearing things."

Chapter Six

ALEX SHOWED UP the next day around noon with two boxes, three large suitcases, a laptop, and Bacon poking his head out of the fancy carrier.

"Wait your turn," Chyna said when Luca tried wrestling the dog away. "He smells so good, Alex."

"I gave him a bath this morning."

"He's adorbs," Chyna crooned, hugging the dog to his chest. "Does he stay in his crate while you're at work?"

"Yes, but I leave it open in case he needs to use the litter box."

"Aren't those only for cats?"

"They work great for tiny dogs as well."

"So...no chance of walking onto a pile of steaming dog shit?" Luca asked.

Alex laughed. "Bacon's piles are tiny enough to pick up with a tissue, and he's been trained since he was eight weeks old. I've never had any problems."

"He sounds too perfect," Luca said. "Doesn't he have any bad doggy habits?"

"No," Alex said, looking offended.

"Seriously, dude. I've had dogs, and I know they don't always follow rules. But this little guy is so cute it'll be easy to forgive."

"Bacon won't disappoint you," Alex promised.

Chyna handed over the dog and watched as he and Luca exchanged sloppy kisses.

"I'll set up his cage and litter box in my room so they won't be in your way," Alex said.

"Why not put the litter box on the balcony?" Chyna suggested.

"I guess we could do that."

Alex sounded reluctant, though, and Luca jumped right in. "It'll be too cold in the winter; let's put the box in the bathroom."

Looking relieved, Alex said, "Actually, that's where I normally keep it, but I wasn't sure you'd be cool with him taking a dump in the bathroom with you."

"That's what bathrooms are for," Luca said practically. "You'll have to be religious about cleaning it, so it doesn't stink up the place."

"That goes without saying, sugar. I would never let Bacon step in a dirty box."

"Then it's settled. Do you need help unpacking?" Chyna offered.

"I'm good," Alex said. "Is it all right if I let Bacon roam around?"

"Are you kidding?" Luca said. "He's got two new fans. Shouldn't we feed him?"

Alex pulled one of the moving boxes apart and plucked out a fancy wrought-iron stand and two ceramic bowls. He filled one with water and poured kibble into the second bowl, placing the stand on the floor near the refrigerator. Bacon trotted over to the familiar sight and chowed down like he'd been doing it forever.

"He's on an open feed method so there's no need to worry if I'm delayed at my job."

"Wow, most dogs would eat themselves into a coma," Luca remarked.

"Not my baby," Alex said affectionately. "He only eats until he's full. Usually twice a day."

While they were watching Bacon, Alex pulled more doggy paraphernalia out of the box in the living room. He set the litter box in the bathroom—next to the toilet—and moved the carry case and cage to his bedroom where he stayed for a while, presumably putting his things away.

"The property manager better not give me a hard time about the dog," Chyna worried. "I would hate to turn away such a nice addition to my life."

"A lot of apartment dwellers have pets," Luca noted. "Why shouldn't you?"

"Because he's obviously an afterthought."

"Alex will charm the pants off him," Luca said.

"I'm glad we picked him," Chyna said. "He's nice."

"Yeah, he's cool," Luca agreed.

"Maybe we should ask him to join us for lunch," Chyna suggested.

"Or not," Luca said. "I have to be at the bus stop in less than four hours, and I'd rather spend them alone with you."

"I wish you didn't have to go."

"That makes two of us, but you'll be making a trip to Ithaca before you know it," Luca said gently. "I feel better leaving you now that you won't be alone."

Chyna drew Luca into a tight embrace. "Promise me you'll call every night."

"You know I will," Luca assured him. He slung his backpack over one shoulder and reached for Chyna's hand. "Come on. Let's grab something to eat."

They said goodbye to Alex, who waved them off with a friendly thumbs-up, and exited the apartment without another thought. In the elevator, Luca pointed out that they were far too trusting.

"We didn't even bother checking his references," Luca mentioned. "You might come home to an empty apartment someday."

"You've been watching too many episodes of *Mr. Robot*, babe. Anyone who names their dog Bacon has to be harmless."

"Good point," Luca said, grinning.

"It'll be interesting to hear his story," Chyna said.

"Why?"

"I mean he's kind of my opposite, isn't he?"

"How do you figure?" Luca asked warily.

"Alex was born in a female body. He probably went through hormone hell and a few surgeries to get this far."

"Uh-huh," Luca responded.

All of a sudden, he wished that Chyna had chosen Xara to be his roommate. On the surface, Alex appeared to be the perfect candidate, but would he be the friend Chyna needed or a constant source of confusion? Since leaving his support system in Illinois, Chyna's gender dysphoria had snuck through at unexpected moments. The childbearing issue was the most recent example. Was he still clinging to the idea of transitioning to female while pretending it had been laid to rest? If that was the case, what was Luca supposed to do? Chip still hadn't returned his call. Perhaps he'd gone away for the long weekend and couldn't be bothered with outside interference, which was common with most people, but not Chip. Luca was his best friend and his twin's boyfriend. Two compelling reasons to pick up the phone.

As casually as possible, Luca asked, "Did Chip and Meghan go anywhere special for Labor Day weekend?"

"I think they're hiking somewhere in the Appalachians," Chyna said.

"You gotta be kidding."

"I know," Chyna said. "Who does that sort of shit?"

"Chip," they both said at the same time and burst out laughing.

They took the subway down to the closest stop near the Cornell Club on East 44th and decided to walk to P.J. Clarke's for burgers on 3rd Avenue at 55th. It wasn't that far a walk, and the iconic eatery had come up first on Luca's search engine when trying to decide where they should go that was close enough to the club so he wouldn't miss his bus ride back to Ithaca.

The atmosphere was old-fashioned but warmly inviting. Once again, the architectural student zeroed in on the distinct signs of a bygone era. Dark wooden ceilings, brick walls covered with signed celebrity photos, checkered red and white tablecloths, and chalkboard menus looked perfectly appropriate, even in this age of fast food and takeout. They were led to a table for two and handed menus.

After a few minutes, Chyna took his eyes off the menu and looked up at Luca in alarm. "Babe, are you prepared to pay twenty bucks for a burger when we can get the same at McDonald's for a fourth of the price?"

"I've never eaten here and my dad's loved it, so yeah, let's splurge."

"Are you sure?"

"We barely spent any money this weekend."

"Because we were otherwise occupied," Chyna said playfully.

"Got that right," Luca said, reaching across the table to squeeze Chyna's hand. "It was the best part of the weekend."

"I love you," Chyna said, staring into his eyes. "So much."

"I know," Luca said. "And I love you a ton back. Now, stop worrying about the bill 'cause this is my treat."

"If you say so," Chyna said, studying the menu again.

"What are you having?" Luca asked when the waiter appeared to take the order.

"Organic turkey burger and sweet potato fries."

Luca made a face. "Seriously?"

"Yeah, I'm sure it'll be fabulous."

"Okay," Luca said, shrugging. "I'll have the Cadillac, medium, and regular fries."

"Drinks?" the waiter asked.

"Dr. Pepper for me and—"

"Iced tea for me," Chyna said.

Luca was dying to share his concerns about Alex with Chyna, but he didn't want to spend the last few hours of their time together bickering over his sudden misgivings. It wasn't fair to Chyna, and certainly not to Alex. Luca would put his misgivings on hold for now and hope to God he was wrong. Chyna would stay his course and reach out to Chip or him if the need arose.

They took their time savoring the delicious food, and afterward, they took a leisurely walk down 57th Street and window-shopped. It seemed like all the big names were clustered on this particular street: Bergdorf Goodman, Bulgari, Burberry, Tiffany, Chanel, Hermes, and Louis Vuitton to name a few. They had almost ninety minutes to spare, so Luca ducked into Niketown and bought a pair of shoes, and then followed Chyna into Victoria's Secret for a few select choices of underwear. At Starbucks, they had coffee and brownies and continued the walk back to the Cornell Club.

Zeb was already waiting at the bus stop, and he waved when he spied Luca and Chyna.

"How's it going?" Luca asked when they reached him.

"Pretty good," Zeb replied. "Did you guys have a nice weekend?"

"It couldn't have been more perfect," Luca said, kissing Chyna on the lips.

"Does this mean I won't hear you complaining about missing your boyfriend for a while?" Zeb asked.

"Nah," Luca replied. "That'll be a constant. Might as well get used to it."

They continued the light bantering until the bus showed up to take them back to school, and after hugs and kisses were passed around, Luca boarded the bus, found a seat, and hunkered down for the journey.

Chapter Seven

I WAS GLOOMY on the way home, already missing Luca. If I planned to survive these regular separations, falling into a pit of despair after each of Luca's visits would be my downfall. As much as I hated the physical distance, modeling had been my choice and learning how to cope had to be my top priority. Whining and complaining would only cause more stress on both sides.

Bacon welcomed me with excited yips and frenzied wagging, hopping up and down, and occasionally pawing at my jeans in case I happened to miss his over-the-top but heartwarming greeting. It certainly beat coming home to an empty apartment. I picked him up and giggled when he bathed my cheeks with exuberant laps that tickled and comforted at the same time. After a few minutes, I put him down, and as the dog scampered toward Alex's room, I decided to check on my new roommate to see how he was settling in.

I knocked on the partially opened door and entered after hearing his melodic, "Come in, sugar."

Pausing at the threshold, I took in the mess. Alex was undoubtedly a fashionista judging by the piles of clothing covering the bed and spilling out of open suitcases. Interestingly, most of the items were black. A number of elegant but somber-colored suits hung in the closet while the ledge above the hanging rod contained a display of hats in varying styles. An impressive array of athletic shoes were lined up beside two rows of casual and evening selections. Boxes that looked like they might contain boots were piled one on top of another.

"Wow," I exclaimed at the huge variety.

Alex smiled sheepishly. "Despite all the therapy in the world, my consummate need to buy something new whenever I'm down in the dumps isn't that easy to extinguish. Nothing makes me feel better than a new pair of shoes."

Chyna laughed. "I guess not. You've got more clothes in here than I've had in my entire life. It's fucking impressive."

"I have zero willpower when it comes to clothes. Do you think I'm a freak?" Alex asked.

"I'm the last one to judge," Chyna admitted.

"There's nothing odd about you from where I'm standing."

"My issues are all here," I said, tapping my head.

"But...you look so normal..." Alex observed, "if the norm were gorgeous men with flaming red hair falling down their backs. I'd sell all my shoes to look like you for an hour."

"Because—"

"You're the whole package," Alex gushed. "Coloring, height, features...I mean, honestly, sugar. What more could you ask for?"

My gaze drifted toward the window. The sun had almost disappeared and city lights were becoming more visible. *What more could you ask for....*

I thought back on all the years I'd longed for boobs and a vagina. People always wanted what they didn't or couldn't have. Turning my attention back to Alex, I asked, "Do you have scars where they removed your breasts?"

Alex narrowed his eyes.

"You asked me what I could possibly want...."

"What's that got to do with my barely lamented boobs?" Alex inquired.

"How old were you when you had the mastectomies?"

Looking more confused than ever, Alex said, "Old enough."

"Any regrets?" I asked.

"None whatsoever," Alex stated. "Do you want to tell me why you're so interested?"

I wished the conversation hadn't veered off in this direction. It wasn't fair to burden Alex with my past when it had no relevance to the present. "I'll share the reason another day, but at the moment, it looks like you can use me for something more productive. How can I help with your unpacking?"

Alex pointed at the bed. "Let's clear that, or I'll have to sleep on the floor."

"Do you hang your jeans or fold them away in a bureau?"

"Honey, I not only hang my jeans, I iron them," Alex said proudly.

"Sheesh...I guess you're still a girl underneath the macho exterior."

Alex dropped a pair of jeans and froze.

I gasped. "Oh my God, I can't believe I said that."

"Neither can I," Alex seethed.

"I'm sorry," I said, taking a step forward. "Please forgive me."

"Do you mean it?" Alex asked. "I've made great strides in my transition, and I don't need my own roommate to be blindsiding me when I least expect it."

I felt sick with remorse. If I didn't share my past right this second, Alex would never forgive me for being so insensitive.

"You asked me a few minutes ago why I was so interested in… your boobs," I said haltingly. "Maybe you won't hate me so much after I explain."

"I don't hate you," Alex said. "I'm disappointed to hear you say something so cruel."

I didn't realize I was crying until Alex gently thumbed away my tears.

"Aw, come on, sugar. Don't cry over me."

I sniffed and reached for Alex's free hand. In a strangled voice, I gave Alex an abridged version of my life. To his credit, Alex didn't interrupt with questions or mouth platitudes. He listened silently until I finished my recitation.

"So you see," I said in conclusion. "The need to fit in with a set of boobs and a functional hoo-ha colored my existence for fifteen years. It was as important to me as your wish to shed all outward traces of your female persona. I should have known better than to throw out such a thoughtless remark."

"I forgive you," Alex said gently. "You've survived your own private hell, and it looks like I'm in the right place after all. Kindred spirits need to stick together. May I ask you a question?"

"Sure."

"Are you happy?"

I looked into Alex's earnest face. There were no signs of ghoulish curiosity or suppressed judgment. All I could see was genuine concern.

"I love Luca and my decision to embrace my male persona was best for both of us. Fortunately, he has no problem with my occasional cross-dressing. I'm totally hung up on ribbons and lace. That's never going to change."

"Neither will my shoe fetish," Alex admitted. "The selection in men's footwear is shockingly limited. I'm seriously thinking of taking up design on the side so I can rectify the problem."

"I totally agree. I'd love to wear a pair of strappy sandals on my way to work, but I'm worried about getting bashed before I catch the train."

"Why do you think half of my clothes are black? I prefer to keep a low profile."

"Can I ask you a question?"

"Go ahead, sugar."

"Do you miss anything about being a girl?"

"Zip," Alex said emphatically. "The only thing I want now is to live an authentic life. I've considered bottom surgery, but there are too many side effects, and I'd rather not risk it."

"Tell me about it," I commiserated. "I researched it to death when I was hoping to transition."

"You don't know how lucky you are to have a penis," Alex said frankly. "Lopping one off is a lot easier than creating one."

"All I wanted to do for years was get rid of it."

"What changed?" Alex asked curiously.

I smirked. "I started using it for something more than peeing."

Alex's belly laugh filled the air and I joined in. It was great to find the humor in something that seemed so earth-shattering a few years ago. With a firm sense of camaraderie, I went to grab a couple of sodas before we resumed our unpacking.

In the middle of sorting his ties, Alex asked, "Why haven't you changed your name?"

I stopped folding clothes. "Why should I?"

"No offense, but I thought you were a woman when Melinda first approached me about sharing the apartment. Chyna is a lovely name, but it brings a female to mind. If you're at peace with your decision, why not put the girl to rest?"

"I like my name," I admitted. "Do you really think it's necessary?"

"When I walked out of that courthouse with my new name, I felt reborn. It was another proactive step in the right direction."

"I'll give it some thought."

Much later, after we'd gone to our respective rooms, Luca called to let me know he'd arrived.

"I miss you already," he said.

"Same here."

"We better get to sleep, or we'll be zombies tomorrow."

"Luca?"

"What, babe?"

"You think I should change my name?"

"Um...do you want to?"

"Alex thinks it'll underscore my decision to move forward as a male."

"How much does Alex know about you?" Luca asked.

"It kind of came out earlier after I said something thoughtless."

"What'd you say?"

I gave Luca a brief rundown on that awful moment when I was sure Alex would pack up and leave. "It was a stupid thing to say," I confessed, getting all weepy again.

Alarmed, Luca asked, "Are you crying?"

I sniffed and choked out an embarrassed laugh. "You're getting the diluted aftermath. I was a wreck earlier."

"I'm sure Alex knows you didn't mean anything spiteful."

"Now he does, but at the time, he thought I was another judgmental asshole."

"Did you clear the air?"

"Yes, we bonded."

"Sounds like it," Luca said. "Is that how the subject of your name came about?"

"Yeah. We traded stories about our journeys from crazy, mixed-up kids to functioning young adults. He seems to think a name change will do me good."

"It's a big decision," Luca remarked. "I would talk to Chip and your dads before you move forward."

"How do you feel about it?"

"I'll support you no matter what."

"That's a PC answer, Luca. What's the truth?"

"You've sort of caught me off guard." Luca said. "I've known you as Chyna or Doll or both for years. Calling you something different will take some getting used to. Did you have a name in mind?"

"No, but the more I think about it, the easier it gets to arrive at a decision. I've spent years pretending to be someone else, policing my gender presentation and mannerisms so I wouldn't raise any suspicions. It was exhausting. Even after I was outed, I was still doing what others expected. For the first time in my life, I can be the most authentic me. The name Chyna is a carryover from another world and a feminine label that's starting to grate. When I show up at a photo shoot, people want to know how I arrived at Chyna. Many think it's a pseudonym, and helping them to connect the dots gets tiresome after a while."

"I had no idea you felt so strongly about this," Luca said.

"Me neither," I admitted. "Alex's story made me realize a few things about my own. It's nice to be able to share my thoughts with someone who relates in many ways."

"I guess so," Luca said, sounding a little hurt.

"He'll never replace you as my soul mate, babe. Not in a million years."

"I hope not."

"Count on it. You'll always be my go-to person in times of crisis. Then Chip. Then both my foster dads. But having Alex around will be nice. I think he can fill the void on the days when I'm missing your shoulder to lean on."

Luca snorted. "Not too well, I hope."

"You have nothing to worry about."

"Going back to the name change," Luca said. "Let's compare lists after a few days."

"Lists?"

"This is a major decision," Luca reminded me. "One you'll live with for the rest of your life. You have to choose something that'll represent the new you as well as stand up to scrutiny."

"So Loki won't do?" I teased.

"No," Luca said, sounding horrified.

His reaction made me giggle. "It'll be interesting to see what you consider appropriate."

Chapter Eight

LUCA MUST HAVE looked puzzled after he disconnected the phone because Zeb asked if there was a problem.

"Is Chyna okay?"

"Yeah," Luca said, frowning. "Except he threw me for a loop with a possible name change."

"Sorry?"

"All of a sudden, Chyna feels his name doesn't suit his personality."

"To be fair, I was a bit confused the first time I heard his name."

"Why?"

"Names that end with the letter A are usually female oriented. Chino would have made more sense."

Luca let out a long sigh. "It's a long story, Zeb, and not really mine to share. Chyna says it's been raising some questions, and he's tired of it."

"What's he going to do?"

"Change it."

"Does he have anything picked out?"

"No, we're each making a list of possible replacements, and then he has to run it by the 'rents."

"Can I throw in a few suggestions?" Zeb asked excitedly.

"As long as they don't start with a Z," Luca joked.

"Don't worry," Zeb assured him. "I like Logan."

Luca started a list on his phone. "Got it."

"What's Chyna's last name?" Zeb asked.

"Davidson."

"That's easy to match."

"You think?"

"Yup. How's Aaron, Adam, Aiden—"

"Stop," Luca said. "We're not going through the fucking alphabet, Zeb. Pick out your favorites—no more than ten—and we'll add them to the list."

"I need to think about this at length," Zeb said. "Chyna deserves something unique."

"No shit," Luca said. "Let's talk about it later."

"When are you seeing him again?"

"Depends on my football schedule."

"Gotcha."

It took Luca over an hour to fall asleep. He was taunted by visions of Chyna and Alex huddled together on the sofa exchanging war stories. He knew he was being completely irrational and had to come to grips with their situation, but it was harder than he'd anticipated.

The following morning, he sent Chyna a love emoticon, and when he got something similar—accompanied by actual words—Luca felt much better. Surrendering to his insecurities, instead of trusting in their love, was no way to live. He'd have to stomp on the urge to pick up the phone or hop on a bus whenever he or Chyna perceived a problem. As much as he loved his guy, Luca had heard it all, multiple times.

Modeling might possibly present a new set of issues, but the ongoing theme was the same. Authenticity was paramount after years of deceit, and Chyna's desire to begin his professional career with a new name shouldn't have come as a big surprise. What confused Luca was the amount of time it took to arrive at the realization.

Shortly after Chyna was outed, a name change had been suggested. He'd dismissed the offer without hesitation, but a lot had happened since then. If his career took off the way Melinda predicted, Chyna would become a celebrity. People would be interested in all aspects of his life including his unusual name. Why not avoid the backstory with a fresh identity?

With that in mind, Luca spent much of his day thinking of and rejecting names. It messed with his concentration, and he spent part of freehand drawing doodling curlicues around letters rather than doing his work. It was like this for most of the day and carried over to football practice. Coach had asked him to stay when drills were over to find out if there was a problem. He was one of four quarterbacks in training, and the one with the most promise, but his commitment to a sport that had been a large part of his formative years had been replaced by his devotion to Chyna. Luca didn't see how he was going to make it all work. He was carrying a full load of classes, which was what he wanted, and with football thrown in the mix, there was no spare time for anything.

With his schedule in hand, he headed back to the dorms and realized with a sinking heart that every weekend was allocated to games. At this rate, he'd never see Chyna. Even Thanksgiving break would be interrupted by football.

Zeb wasn't back yet, and Luca decided to Skype with his dads to discuss his concerns.

"Dad," he said when the familiar face appeared on screen.

"Hey, buddy. How's it going?"

Luca could see the kitchen in the background and Lil, his stepfather, standing behind his biological father, Grier, with a white apron around his waist.

"Am I interrupting dinner?"

"Not yet, sweetie. How are you?" Lil asked.

"Confused."

"About what?" Grier asked.

"Football," Luca announced. "What'll happen if I quit?"

"You're not on an athletic scholarship, so no one's going to throw you out of school if that's what you're worried about," Lil said.

"Would you be disappointed in me?" Luca addressed Grier. "You've always taught me to finish what I start, no matter what, but you know I was on the fence about college football. Now, more than ever, I realize there's no way to make this work without jeopardizing something. I won't reduce my workload, and I'm not giving up any free time I might have to spend with Chyna."

Grier frowned. "So this is all about your boyfriend."

"Sweetie, you did say you'd try football for a year," Lil reminded him. "I understand you need to be with Chyna as often as possible, but you're only in college once. There won't be any do-overs. You have the rest of your life to be together."

"You can't know that for sure," Luca said stubbornly. "What if he meets someone better than me? He's going to be surrounded by beautiful people, and I'm too far away to do anything about it."

"Oh, Luca," Lil sympathized. "No one compares to you."

"You're biased."

"Perhaps, but I'm also a man with twenty-twenty vision."

"With your contacts," Grier teased.

Lil gave him a withering look. "Don't remind me."

"Guys," Luca said. "You're getting off topic."

"As I was saying before I was so rudely interrupted," Lil said, turning back to the camera. "Aside from being good-looking, you're intelligent, hardworking, and thoughtful. Plus, you're embarking on a fabulous career. One day, you'll be able to give Chyna the moon if that's what he wants. He'd never throw you over for a momentary distraction. You're a keeper, sweetie."

"Thanks, Daddio. I still maintain you're totally biased, but it's nice to hear the praise. Still, I want to be with Chyna every chance I get. Staying on the football team will make it impossible."

"I hate to play devil's advocate," Grier broke in, "but if Chyna's going to cheat on you, it'll happen no matter what you do."

"That's not helpful, Dad."

"Look, I don't mean to burst your bubble, kiddo, but you have to trust each other," Grier said. "You can't put your life on hold on the off chance you won't be around to beat off the bad guys. Give Chyna more credit and stop acting like an insecure child. You're way past that stage."

Luca was stunned by Grier's disapproval. He wanted to lash out and say something insulting, but it would only confirm his father's opinion that he'd regressed and turned into an insecure dweeb.

Luca cleared his throat. "You've made your point. I'll try to bury my fears, be less clingy, and a lot more mature, but the football schedule is still a problem. I'm not interested in playing."

"Then quit," Grier snapped.

"It's not like I'm backing out midseason," Luca rationalized. "We haven't even played our first game. Isn't it better to do it now and give the coaches time to prepare someone else?"

"Luca, you know there's nothing I enjoy more than watching you play football," Lil interjected. "But you'll be doing the team a disservice if your heart's not in the game. Quitting is the responsible thing to do. Your coach might not be happy tomorrow, but he'd be furious if you did it further into the season."

"See?" Luca said, trying to get Grier to cave. "Daddio gets it."

Grier smirked. "You've had Daddio wrapped around your little finger since you were six years old. He'll always be on your side."

"I don't understand why you're being such a di...I mean, Dad, come on," Luca said plaintively. "Don't you remember what it's like to be in love?"

Lil grabbed Grier's hand, and Luca watched as they stared at each other, silently communicating like they'd been doing for years. Luca could tell his father was taking this badly, and he waited, not daring to interrupt whatever was happening between his fathers. Finally, Grier turned back to Luca.

"I'm still in love," Grier said in a conciliatory tone. "For a second, I forgot what it was like in the early days of our relationship. We agonized over separations as well and it sucked. Go ahead and talk to your coach. He'll appreciate your honesty."

"Thanks, Dad," Luca said. "I'll do my best to make you proud in other ways."

"Luca, you've never disappointed me," Grier said. "Daddio and I couldn't be prouder."

"He's right, sweetie."

"Even today?"

Grier nodded. "Especially today. Standing up to me took guts, and I might not agree with your decision, but I trust your instincts. If you feel this is best for you overall, then you have my blessing."

Luca felt his throat tighten, and tears were already starting to form. He refused to give in to his emotions and confirm Grier's opinion that he was immature.

"I love you both," he said quickly. "Thank you for listening and being supportive."

He shut the laptop before they could respond and reached for something to wipe his cheeks.

When Zeb walked in twenty minutes later, Luca had regained his composure.

"Have you had dinner?" Zeb asked, throwing a small pile of books down on his desk.

"Nope. Want to grab a pizza or something?" Luca asked.

"That would be great," Zeb said, heading back out.

Over dinner, Zeb threw out some more names for Luca to add to the growing list. He'd chosen most of them from *The Vampire Diaries*, a show Luca barely watched.

"Dude, I can't imagine Chyna liking the name Alaric. It sounds like a laxative."

Zeb frowned. "How about Damon or Stefan?"

"Doesn't go with Davidson."

"Jeremy? That totally goes with his last name. Or even Tyler."

"I'll put it on the list," Luca said. "You can only add five more."

"Hey, that's two."

"I included the first three names that started with A."

"Delete them," Zeb said.

Luca rolled his eyes but reached for his phone. "I'm getting rid of Aaron, Adam, and Aiden."

"Wait," Zeb said. "Leave Adam on the list."

"Because...?"

"Rock star, dude."

"You like Adam Lambert?"

"And your point is?" Zeb said.

Luca shrugged.

"Hey, we've got our elective on Thursday. Didn't you tell me you also signed up for Visual Imaging?"

"Yeah, I'm looking forward to it," Luca said.

"Me too."

"By the way," Luca said, "I'm quitting the football team tomorrow."

"How come?" Zeb asked, confused. "I thought you loved the game."

"There's not enough time for everything I want to do."

"Maybe we'll be able to hang out more?"

"Sure," Luca said. "When I'm not with Chyna."

Chapter Nine

MY NEXT MODELING assignment was for a line of hair products. They'd been expecting a female, given my name and headshot, and whoever was in charge hadn't done their homework properly as my gender was clearly stated in my profile. The collective gasps when I walked through the door in acid-washed jeans, motorcycle boots, and a Diesel T-shirt reinforced Alex's suggestion.

Mel came to my rescue, pointing out *Cover Girl* and their groundbreaking ad featuring a male model. Having me stand out as the only male redhead—among the clutch of females in varying shades of blonde, brunette, and silver—would be a plus rather than a minus. By the time she was done arguing, they were totally on board with her plan and couldn't wait to see what sort of hype their ad would generate.

I listened as one executive after another voiced their opinion while casting glances my way. The photographer sided with Mel, raving about my hair and ability to appeal to both male and female customers. They were discussing me like I wasn't even here. It made me feel like an item on a grocery shelf they were inspecting from different angles. I loved being the center of attention, but to be in the spotlight for misleading a client due to my name was irritating. I pulled out my phone and sent Luca a text.

Me: name change imperative
Luca: what happened?
Me: clients expecting a girl mucho drama
Luca: did you get the job?
Me: think so
Luca: any name ideas? Zeb has Adam, Jeremy, and Taylor
Me: don't like those
Luca: I looked up names for gingers in other countries
Me: ?
Luca: Rory, Reed, Russ, Flynn

Me: Flynn iz coo
Luca: yeah?
Me: let me run it by Mel
Luca: your name!?!
Me: still need to discuss
Luca: can I see you this weekend?
Me: going to Miami for a shoot
Luca: ☹
Me: sucks
Luca: how long?
Me: I dunno maybe 4 days
Luca: next weekend?
Me: I gotta check
Luca: k later
Me: luv u
Luca: me 2

Mel signaled and I approached the client, enduring another inspection. Now I felt like a slab of meat as they twirled me this way and that, checking out my best angle, asking repeatedly if my hair color was real or store-bought. When I swore it was the real deal, they exclaimed in delight as they brushed the long strands. They sold shampoos and conditioners, after all, so hair was their thing and I accepted the praise. By now, I was certain they'd hire me. If they could credit their products for my healthy hair, people would be grabbing their bottles off the shelf.

Now they were talking about flying us to Hawaii for the shoot. Why they couldn't recreate a rain forest in a studio given all their resources was unclear, but the idea of traveling was exciting. I'd never been anywhere before landing in New York, and now Mel was talking future trips to Miami and Honolulu. And this was only the beginning. If my career took off, I would most likely be seeing parts of Europe next.

The idea of traveling to Paris for the first time without Luca was upsetting, though. I couldn't imagine being in such a romantic city without him by my side. I'd been surprised, and felt a little guilty, when Luca told me he quit football to be able to spend more time with me. I wondered if Lil and Grier were upset. Would they blame me for Luca's decision? The sad part was I couldn't put my career on hold whenever Luca wanted to visit. He should have run it by me first, but Luca had taken the drastic step on his own. He'd insisted it had more to do with his lack of interest in the sport than anything else. I wasn't sure that was true.

As for getting together more often, the next few months would be challenging, judging by our most recent text. At this rate, we'd be climbing the walls by the time we saw each other again. Maybe I could sneak in a visit to Ithaca before leaving for Hawaii.

As we were leaving the studio, I asked Mel if we could have lunch. She'd be going back to Chicago in a few days, and I wanted to iron out some concerns. She suggested a fusion-type café close by, and after placing our orders—a Cobb salad for me and a burger for Mel—the waiter took away the menus, and I opened the conversation with a question.

"Did you change your legal name when you transitioned?"

"Of course," Mel said. "Do I look like a Melvin to you?"

"God no. I would have changed it regardless."

She barked out a laugh. "I couldn't wait to get rid of it. Why are you bringing this up now?"

"You saw what happened back there. This isn't the first time my name has misled people into thinking they're dealing with a female."

"Now that you mention it, there have been some questions raised, but I was hesitant to say anything since you seemed determined to hang on to Chyna," Mel remarked.

"I'm starting to realize a name change might make my life easier. There's nothing worse than starting out on the wrong foot, and digging myself out of the box they've carefully constructed around me is getting redundant. What do you think of Flynn?"

"It goes well with Davidson," Mel said. "Does it mean anything special?"

"Luca says it's used for gingers."

Mel googled the name and found the source. "It's an Irish surname transferred to forename use from an Anglicized version of Gaelic ó floinn, meaning descendant of Flann, which means red or ruddy. I thought you didn't like being called Red."

"I don't like Red, but Flynn is pretty cool."

"What are your other choices?"

"Rory, Russ, Reed. They're all about red or rosy in one form or another. Nothing has grabbed me as much as Flynn," I admitted. "Honestly, this just came up a few days ago after my conversation with Alex."

"How's that working out?"

"I like him a lot."

"We've never actually met even though I referred him. He's a trans guy, right?"

"Uh-huh. You must not have met him because he's unforgettable," I pointed out. "He's the one who broached the subject of changing my name."

"It sounds like you guys have bonded in a short time."

"We're a good fit."

"Does Luca like him?" Mel asked.

"Of course."

"I'm surprised he let a guy move in."

"Let?"

"Luca is extremely territorial."

"So am I," I confessed. "Imagining Luca with anyone else makes me crazy."

"I wouldn't worry about your boyfriend, Chyna. I've never met anyone as devoted as him."

"Don't you like him?" I asked.

"Why would you say that?"

"You seem critical all of a sudden."

"That's not the case," Mel said. "I was merely making an observation. He watches you like a hawk."

"We worry about each other," I defended. "That's not a bad thing."

"Getting back to your name change," Mel said. "Do you mind if I throw in my two cents' worth?"

"This is why we're sitting here," I said pointedly. "Do I need anyone's permission to legally change my name?"

"No, you're nineteen, so there shouldn't be a problem," Mel replied. "I want you to think about this decision. Your name will be your brand and will follow you long after you've quit modeling. Rory is cute for a nineteen-year-old, but not for a thirty- or forty-year-old. You want to choose something that will withstand the test of time."

"You do agree that it's necessary?" I asked.

"Absolutely."

"Okay. I'll keep you posted, and meanwhile, if you would double check on the legalities, I'd appreciate it."

"No problem. Anything else?"

"How much time do I have between Miami and Hawaii?"

"Hawaii isn't on the books yet. Figure a week or so."

"Can I go and visit Luca?"

"Sure, but be back in plenty of time. You want to establish a reputation as a reliable and hard-working model. It doesn't matter how beautiful you are, kiddo. If your work ethic sucks, they'll shy away from you like you've got herpes."

"Gross."

"It's the truth. Time is money, and problem models are replaced on the daily. You don't want to be that guy."

"I hear you loud and clear."

"One more thing," Mel said. "They want to wax off all your body hair for the hair shoot."

"Excuse me?"

"Bare chest down to a few inches above your groin. Armpits and legs as well."

"I'm not modeling a bathing suit, am I?"

"No."

"Then why?"

"To keep the whole androgynous thing going. Excessive body hair is too masculine."

"I'm a guy."

"Yes, but they want you to blend in with the other models."

"That's idiotic."

"It's a marketing ploy, Chyna. No disrespect intended."

"Waxing will hurt like hell, and when it grows back, I'll die of the itch. Being natural was the best part of shedding my female persona."

"I know it's a pain in the ass, but this is your job."

"Luca will be furious."

"He's not signing the check," Mel reminded me. "You're either in or out of this career, Chyna. You'll be asked to do stranger things in the future, and I need to be sure I won't get any negative feedback."

"What weird things?"

"Body paint or they might ask you to model female PJs or underwear."

I blinked several times, trying to take it all in. "Seriously?"

"It's like acting. You do what they ask."

"I'm not sleeping with anyone."

Looking outraged, Mel leaned forward. "Did I mention sex at any time?"

"No, and it's a good thing too."

"I'm not your pimp, and I resent the implication."

"I'm sorry," I said immediately. "You've always had my back."

"Damn right! My job is to keep you safe but also to make sure we do everything right to get you to the top. That doesn't include sex or drugs. You stay away from anyone who suggests one or the other."

"You've made your point, and let me apologize once more. I'm sorry for suggesting you'd be anything but above board. Now, can we change the subject?"

"Sure."

"Don't book me around Thanksgiving."

"Why not?" Mel asked, leaning forward.

"I'm going home with Luca."

"I'll do my best," Mel said. "Once more, I have to remind you of priorities. We try not to schedule anyone around the big holidays, but once in a while, it's inevitable."

"Please?" I begged. "I want to see my family."

Mel nodded. "I'll work on it."

Chapter Ten

DAYS FLEW BY as I was thrust headlong into my new career. The idealized vision of modeling I'd entertained before arriving on the scene was quickly replaced by constant reality checks. There was no such thing as an eight-hour day, and privacy was only a word in the dictionary. Models were as much a commodity as the products we were promoting. The tribe of hairdressers, makeup artists, and wardrobe consultants were in charge of transforming me into a spectacular apparition by the time I stood in front of the camera. It took a professional's deft hand to hide tiny facial imperfections, tame the curls, and work magic with eye shadows and lip liners to direct the consumer's gaze in whichever direction the client chose. Sometimes, it was one specific feature—eyes, hands, hair, legs—that needed to be spotlighted, and it was their job to figure out how best to do it.

Mel had set me straight from the beginning and a good thing too. When I first sat in her makeup chair, I'd been presenting as a female and under the misconception I could get away with the charade indefinitely. She'd warned me that nudity was par for the course in the industry, and thinking I could hide behind locked doors to change outfits was ludicrous.

This morning, they'd carted me off to the esthetician—fancy name for a sadistic waxing monster—who'd ordered me to strip and lie down on a table, where she methodically removed every hair on my body, save for a tiny clump around my groin I'd insisted on keeping. It had been pure torture, and what made it worse was the look of contempt on the technician's face each time I yelped when the wax strip was yanked off. The witch had asked me if she could do my balls as well, adding she'd throw in my lightly furred ass if I stopped whining. I was encouraged to consider the offer since I was already laid out like a frog on a dissecting table.

I clutched the face towel that covered my pubes. "Touch me down there and I swear to God the next scream you hear will be yours."

The woman's sneer was infuriating. Was this waxing nightmare going to be a part of my life indefinitely? Mel had encouraged me to keep my androgynous look as it was currently in high demand, and jobs would flow unchecked if I could represent male and female lines. If I insisted on primarily male shoots, I might get away with retaining my body hair, but there would also be a lot of missed opportunities.

I planned to discuss it with Alex later. We'd fallen into a comfortable routine now that secret fears and future dreams had been uncovered. United in our goal to keep ourselves grounded, we worked hard to create a normal home environment. The alternative—falling into the entitled mindset prevalent amongst the superstars—was a sure path to destruction. Models were inherently narcissistic to begin with, and it wouldn't take much for the daily flattery to go to our heads. The constant ego boost usually led to more damaging forms of entertainment such as drugs and alcohol. A toke here, a snort there, a few shots of tequila or vodka to speed along the process and, voila, an addict of some kind was born. Throw in rampant body image issues and it was easy to turn into a hot mess. Ordinary tasks such as bill paying, cooking, cleaning, walking the dog, and taking out the trash were necessary to keep life real.

After a few of my botched attempts in the kitchen, Alex had offered to take over the cooking when he was in town. He came from a family of restaurateurs and was far better equipped than I'd ever be. Feeling guilty was counterproductive, he remarked after another of my spectacular failures ended up in the trash. I could repay his kindness in other ways. Folding and putting away laundry was something I did well, and I often did a few loads for both of us to make up the deficit.

I stirred through tonight's offering listlessly. Alex's chicken dish was delicious, and would have been devoured in record time, except my skin was on fire from the waxing. They'd slathered on some sort of lotion to soothe the burn, but I could still feel the ravaged tissue protesting when I moved. Even the brush of soft cotton against my chest felt uncomfortable.

Bacon did his usual jig when he heard Alex's key turning the lock. He scampered out of the room, and a few moments later, Alex strolled in with his pup snuggled against his chest.

"Hey, sugar," he said, putting Bacon down and pulling out a chair. "How's the food?"

"Fantastic."

"Then why isn't your plate empty?"

I sighed and pushed my meal toward Alex. "You want it? I've barely touched it, and it's still warm."

Alex reached for my plate. "What's the matter?"

I lifted my T-shirt to show off the angry red spots covering my chest.

"Christ!" he exclaimed. "What happened?"

"They turned me into a hairless *thing*."

"Wax?"

"Yeah."

"You must be allergic or something. I've been waxed myself and never reacted like that. Why don't we call your doctor dad and ask him what we should do?"

"I didn't even think of that."

"No sense wasting money at the emergency room when he can diagnose this for free."

"No kidding." I sent Jody a text to see if he was free to Skype. A few minutes later, I got an affirmative reply.

"Can you grab my laptop, please? It hurts to move."

"No prob," Alex said, standing. "Is this rash all over your body?"

"Except for my privates."

"Good thing you didn't let them touch down there."

"No shit. The technician offered to wax my balls, and I told her to keep away or else."

"You're obviously sensitive to the wax or lotion."

"Remind me not to ever do this again."

"Why did you?"

"They insisted. We're posing naked from the waist up with our hair as our only accessory. I guess my peach fuzz wasn't pleasing to the eye."

"They're going to be disappointed when you show up with red dots all over your chest. That's the next stage in this waxing fiasco."

"Can they fire me?"

"This is on them, not you," Alex said reassuringly. "Have you already signed a contract?"

"Uh-huh."

"Then they can't do shit," Alex said. "They'll have to wait until the rash fades."

"How long does that take?"

"I have no idea; ask your dad."

"God, what a disaster," I murmured, turning on the laptop and connecting to my foster father. From the beginning, Clark and Jody had made it clear they had no intention of usurping our father's role, and as such, they'd asked us—Chip and me—to call them by their given names. It raised our comfort level, and the transition from biological to foster parents was a lot more palatable.

"What's going on?" Jody asked the moment we connected.

"Hi, Jody," I deadpanned. "Nice to see you too."

"I'm sorry, Chyna. I'm having one of those days. How are you?"

"At the moment, I look like I've come down with a raging case of measles."

Jody peered into the computer screen. "Show me."

I got as close to the camera as possible. After a few seconds, I moved back so I could see Jody's face.

"What happened today?" he asked diplomatically.

I recounted the waxing debacle and Alex's amateur diagnosis.

"Your roommate's correct," Jody said. "You appear to be having some kind of allergic reaction. What's the name and address of the closest pharmacy?"

"Hold on," I said. "Alex is googling pharmacies right now."

"There's a Duane Reade close by that's open 24 hours," Alex informed Jody. "Do you want the number?"

"Yes, please," Jody replied.

Alex rattled off the information, and Jody wrote it down before addressing Alex again.

"Thanks for your help, Alex. I'm Jody Williams, by the way, Chyna's foster father."

"You're welcome, sir. Nice to meet you."

"Likewise. Chyna, can you get to the pharmacy tonight?"

I turned to Alex. "Want to go for a walk?"

"Sure," Alex said. "It's only eight."

"All right. I'm calling in a prescription for the highest dose of Benadryl. If I were there, I'd give you a shot, but this is the next best thing. Follow the directions that the pharmacist will include with the script. I'm also adding some lotion to help with the pain and skin discoloration."

"How soon will the spots disappear?" I asked.

"Twenty-four to thirty-six hours."

"No," I wailed. "I have a photo shoot tomorrow."

"You're not going to work. The pills will make you drowsy, and the best thing for you is rest. Furthermore, your skin won't be back to normal yet."

"My client will be furious."

"Call Melinda and have her deal with it."

"Okay. Thanks, Jody."

"You're welcome, kiddo. Let me know if things get any worse."

I froze. "Worse?"

"If you develop a fever or the rash stays."

"Oh, okay. I'm not going to get an infection or anything, am I?"

"No, but do me a favor. Next time they offer to wax off your hair, mention this incident. They should do a skin test to see how you'll react to any of the products they use."

"In other words, never use this aloe cream again."

"The wax needs to be tested as well," Jody said. "There are several kinds, you know."

"And you know this how?"

Jody gave me the look that meant drop it.

"Right." I acknowledged his unspoken rebuke. "I'd better get to the pharmacy."

"Be careful," Jody said. "Good night, Alex."

"Good night, sir."

I shut the laptop. "That's that, I guess."

"Your dad's kind of hot."

"Oh God. Please don't tell me you have daddy issues."

"No, but strong, professional types are appealing."

"Let's go before this gets too weird."

"You'd better call Melinda and give her the good news."

"Fuck, she'll have a fit."

Mel was sympathetic but, at the same time, all business. Not exactly what I was hoping for.

"Are you sure you can't camouflage the mess with makeup?"

"Jody said I should stay home regardless."

"He's not your agent," Mel countered. "The client is paying you an astronomical amount of money to show up in good condition."

"Not my fault they ruined me."

"Most models handle waxing without a problem."

"I guess I'm that special snowflake that defies the odds."

"Sarcasm is the last thing I need at this point," Mel said tersely. "Let me do some damage control. Meanwhile, put calamine lotion on your chest."

"Alex and I were about to leave for the pharmacy."

"Call me tomorrow and give me an update."

"Fine."

Alex looked down at Bacon. "Want to go walkies, baby?"

The pup took off and was back in less than a minute with a bright red leash attached to a collar dangling from his mouth. Alex bent down and got him situated, and we headed toward the pharmacy.

It was almost nine at night by the time we made our way back home. There was a definite chill in the air, and I pulled up my hoodie and tucked my hands in my pockets. I regretted leaving my beanie and gloves behind. Frigid ears and fingertips were a vivid reminder that winter was around the corner. As we got closer to home, I spotted the homeless person again, the same one I'd seen in the distance the night Luca and I had gone to the Empire State Building. The clink of bottles and cans rattling around in his wobbly cart made me a little sick to my stomach. Was he warm enough? Where would someone like that sleep?

"Will you think I'm a sap if I give that guy a few bucks?"

"Which guy?" Alex asked.

"The one up ahead."

"It's your choice, sugar."

I asked him to hold Bacon in his arms. "I don't want him freaking out if that person decides to pet him."

"Bacon will bark, not bite."

"Still, we don't want him disturbing the entire neighborhood."

"Go on then," Alex said. "I've got my eye on you in case."

"In case what?"

"He grabs you?"

"Don't be silly."

"Being vigilant is more like it," Alex said darkly.

I assumed Alex had a good reason to be cautious, and maybe one day he'd share it, but I doubted this man was any kind of threat to either of us. He was hunched over the cart handles, practically leaning on them for support, and each step seemed more difficult than the next. As I got closer, my gaze fell on his shoes. They were worn-out sandals. Hardly fit for walking, especially in this climate. I reached into my pocket and pulled out a twenty-dollar bill.

"Hey," I said softly. "Hold up."

He stopped. "Don't hurt me" came a feeble voice from within the folds of a frayed jacket. "I'm just trying to make a few bucks."

"I have no intention of hurting you," I explained gently. "Take this and get something warm to eat. Is there a shelter where you can spend the night?"

Without raising his head, the guy snatched the bill out of my hand. Despite the distance, I got a whiff of stale booze, smoke, and pungent body odor.

"Thanks," he murmured.

"You're welcome."

Instead of heading back, I stood rooted to the spot, wishing I could do more. "Try to get into a shelter."

"So they can rob what little I have?"

"Aren't they supposed to be safe places?"

Instead of answering, the man let out a snort that changed to a hacking cough. He bent over, gasping and choking, trying to dislodge whatever was causing him to lose his breath. The struggle was real and gave me goose bumps. It wouldn't surprise me if he had bronchitis or pneumonia, considering his rough existence. I turned away and headed toward Alex who was frowning in concern.

"Creeped out?" he asked.

"Totally," I replied, shuddering. "Let's go home."

The coughing died down as we entered the confines of the warm lobby. I tried to figure out what prompted my sudden need to play the Good Samaritan. Alex must have had the same thought because he ventured an opinion.

"That was nice of you, sugar, but you have to promise not to do it again unless I'm around to watch your back."

"You think he's dangerous?"

"I don't know, but it's better to be cautious. There's no telling what he'll do, especially now that he knows you're an easy touch."

"Okay," I promised. "I'll keep that in mind."

Chapter Eleven

ON SKYPE, LUCA stared at the fiery rash covering Chyna's torso. His knee-jerk reaction was anger at the person who'd allowed this to happen, but Chyna needed support not criticism.

"Ow, that looks painful," he said instead. "Does it hurt?"

"It feels like a sunburn," Chyna said, "but Jody called in a prescription earlier so it should help. Apparently, I'm having an allergic reaction to the wax or the lotion they used afterward."

"That sucks, babe. Does this mean you're postponing the trip to Miami?"

"It's not my call. Mel will let me know tomorrow."

"If you stay in town, I'd like to visit."

"That'll be nice."

"Get some rest," Luca said gently.

"The Benadryl is supposed to knock me out," Chyna said. He let out a jaw-cracking yawn and grinned. "I guess it's already working. Better go before I face-plant. I love you."

"Love you too." Luca kissed his fingertips and tapped the screen. If they weren't so damn far apart, he'd be able to do more than send a pretend kiss, but for now, he'd have to settle for this. After disconnecting, he put his laptop away and stretched out on the bed. Zeb had been quietly reading throughout the conversation with Chyna and finally commented.

"Dude, he should get compensated by the client for pain and suffering."

"Right? Although there's probably some CYA clause somewhere in the contract."

"What does that mean?"

"Cover your ass."

"More than likely," Zeb agreed. "Are models obligated to do whatever their clients ask?"

"If the assignment calls for it," Luca said. "Any objections should be addressed before the contracts are signed. No one could have predicted this reaction to the waxing, but it pisses me off when anything bad happens to my guy. He's had more than his share of bad luck."

"At least you'll get to see him this weekend."

"If he's in town," Luca fumed.

"It's obvious you hate this whole modeling gig," Zeb remarked. "Why don't you tell Chyna to quit?"

"Have you ever been in a relationship?" Luca asked incredulously.

"No."

"That explains it."

"Dude, I'm looking for answers," Zeb countered. "Aren't you lying by holding back your true feelings?"

"Chyna knows how I feel, but I would never tell him what he can or can't do."

"You can suggest."

"Yeah, but I've watched my dad's compromise for years, and they have a great marriage. Learning how to be accommodating is as important as love if you want to stay together."

"Okay, Dr. Phil. Aside from being miles apart, why do you dislike his career so much? Are you worried he'll cheat or something?"

"It's crossed my mind," Luca admitted. "But a lot of it stems from being apart for the first time. Chyna's not that kind of guy, and I'm working on my jealous streak. My biggest fear is that people might take advantage of him because he's too eager to please."

"Does this have anything to do with the name thing?"

"Actually, it does."

"Want to talk about it?" Zeb offered. "I'm a good listener."

"It's not my story to tell."

"If it's keeping you up at night...."

"It's not," Luca assured him. "Chyna will tell you one day."

"Okay."

The next morning, Luca got a text letting him know the trip to Miami was off, which meant a visit to the city was a go. He texted back and asked if Zeb could come along and was given the all-clear.

They caught the last bus on Friday afternoon. As soon as they got to the apartment, Luca made the intros between Zeb and Alex and went to check on the patient.

Facedown, Chyna was wearing pajama bottoms and nothing else. Toeing off his shoes, Luca ditched his jeans and shirt but left his boxers on. He slid in gently, hoping Chyna wouldn't wake up, but he must have been half asleep because he rolled over and murmured, "You're here."

"I just got in," Luca said. He eyeballed Chyna's torso and was relieved to see that the red marks had faded somewhat. Not quite photo ready but getting there. "Your rash looks much better."

"Does it?" Chyna asked. "I haven't checked since I passed out last night."

"Alex told me you're taking this way too personally," Luca scolded softly. "Do you want to talk about it?"

Tears welled almost immediately, and Chyna bit down on his quivering lower lip.

"Hey, don't cry," Luca pleaded. "We'll figure this out together."

"What if they fire me?"

"They can't do that," Luca said with certainty.

"Are you sure?"

"You're under contract and it would cost them big bucks to get rid of you."

"I should have listened to my gut when they suggested waxing, but I was worried it would be one more thing they'd hold against me."

"What are you talking about?"

"You know. The confusion surrounding my name."

"This name thing is a load of crap," Luca grumbled, "but what do I know? I'm a college student, not a mover and shaker. In my unsophisticated opinion, a model—or anyone else for that matter—should have the right to call themselves anything they want."

"Maybe I'm hung up on labels since they've been chasing me all my life."

"I get that part, but I don't want you to make such a drastic decision unless it's for yourself. Once you start changing for a job, you lose your identity."

"When did you get so smart?"

Luca snickered. "Didn't you say I was your champion? Anyone who hurts you answers to me."

"My hero," Chyna voiced. "Let me go brush my teeth so I can give you a real kiss."

"Meanwhile, I'll check on Zeb."

Zeb and Alex were seated at the kitchen table when Luca wandered in. He opened the fridge and pulled out a can of Dr. Pepper. "You guys doing okay?"

Alex nodded. "We're fine, sugar. How's Chyna?"

"He'll be better in the morning."

"Make sure he takes another pill before you go to sleep."

"Copy that," Luca said. "Where are they?"

"On his nightstand."

"Got any junk food? I'm starving."

"We don't have junk," Alex said in mock horror, "but there's homemade cookies in that ceramic jar on the counter. Help yourself."

"What kind?"

"Snickerdoodles."

Luca reached in and pulled one out. Taking a bite, he rolled his eyes and let out an orgasmic moan.

Alex grinned. "You're welcome."

He swallowed the rest of the cookie in two bites and reached in for a few more to take back to the bedroom. Wrapping them in a paper towel, he snagged a bottle of water for Chyna before walking out.

Chyna was standing in front of the closet when he walked in with his hands full.

"Whatcha got?"

"Sustenance," he said, handing over the water and cookies.

"Alex is the best thing that's come into my life in a long time," Chyna commented. "I'd be skin and bones without his nurturing."

"Remind me to hug him tomorrow," Luca commented. "Have a cookie and then take a pill so we can move on to...shenanigans."

Chyna chomped down on the cookie with relish. Finished, he popped in the pill and tipped his head back, taking long pulls of water while Luca watched. There was something so fundamentally sexy about a bobbing Adam's apple, especially when the guy had hair halfway down his back and was wearing candy-striped navy and pink pajama bottoms with a glittery pink drawstring.

Luca stood there, transfixed, unable to take his eyes off the man he'd been in love with since he was fifteen. As irrational as it might seem, the thought that anyone, even if it was work related, had laid hands on Chyna and hurt him filled him with such impotent rage he wanted to break something. Instead, he pushed down his boxers, encouraged when

Chyna smiled and pushed down his own pants. The rash was almost gone, leaving a rosy hue over the denuded area. Chyna's auburn love trail that Luca was so fond of was waxed clean, and he couldn't stop himself from letting out a soft curse as he took in the full measure of the manscaping. He sighed in relief when he surveyed the closely trimmed but relatively unscathed bush. Chyna placed his hands on top of Luca's shoulders.

"It'll grow back."

"Eventually." Luca pouted. "I loved your fur."

They were standing in front of the mirrored closet door. Although an inch shorter, Luca was broader, and when he wrapped his arms around Chyna's waist and turned him, so they were both facing the mirror, the illusion that he was taller was enhanced. He swallowed convulsively, mesmerized by their image. The marked contrast in coloring—bronze against ivory—was at once beautiful and erotic.

Chyna flipped his long hair over his chest and leaned against Luca, turning his head and meeting Luca halfway as he captured him in a kiss. Tongues explored soft corners, and warm breaths and saliva commingled with soft cries of pleasure. Luca's right hand slid down past the flat plane of Chyna's stomach and curled around the warm cock that rose up to meet him, the dewy tip poking through the foreskin enticingly.

He spread the natural lube around in slow circles as his own cock lengthened, pressing against the soft fuzz on Chyna's butt. Luca spun Chyna around and lifted him up easily. Arms and legs locked into place, Luca shuffled toward the bed, never taking his mouth off Chyna who was making desperate mewling sounds.

When his shins bumped the edge of the mattress, he laid Chyna down gently. Balancing most of his weight on his elbows, he settled into his place between Chyna's thighs, and they picked up where they'd left off, devouring each other with openmouthed kisses while humping and grinding until they were desperate.

"Let me fuck you," Luca begged. "Please."

Chyna reached for the lube under his pillow and handed it to Luca who prepped them both.

"Ready?" Luca asked, staring into smoldering blue eyes.

"Yes," Chyna said, thrusting up as Luca sank into his body.

Luca's possessive growl reverberated in the quiet room as he pumped in and out. What he lacked in experience was made up in enthusiasm, and Chyna met his eager thrusts with gyrating hips and loud gasps, letting him know he was on the right track. Luca reached for Chyna's cock, which was trapped in between them, to lend him a hand, and Chyna bucked and writhed under his touch.

"I can't hold on," Chyna said.

"Me neither," Luca panted, too far gone to even try. The slow burn had escalated into a five-alarm fire, and they were both going up in the flames of their impending orgasms. After giving one final thrust, Luca unloaded in hot spurts, followed in seconds by Chyna who came with a loud gasp.

"Oh my fucking God," Luca murmured, collapsing against Chyna's damp neck. "That was so worth the wait. I love you."

Chyna's arms tightened around Luca's neck. "I love you too."

They dozed for a while, and when Luca awoke, he went to get a warm washcloth to clean up their mess. Chyna patted his head while Luca was wiping dried cum off his stomach. "Good boy," he said sleepily. "I think I'll keep you."

Luca snorted. "You're getting up next time."

"Deal."

Chapter Twelve

"HEY," LUCA WHISPERED into his phone, glancing to his right to see if the incoming call had disturbed Chyna. He was facing the opposite way, and the even breaths meant he was still down for the count. Luca carefully lifted the sheet and slid out of bed. He was eager to talk to Chip who was finally returning his call after ignoring him for days. He stepped into his boxers and headed for the living room.

"Where the hell have you been?" Luca asked. "I have a ton of stuff to run by you."

"Sorry. My phone broke and it took forever to get a replacement. What's going on?" Chip asked. "Is Chyna in trouble?"

"No, but he's thinking of changing his name."

"What for?"

"Work. Apparently, there's been some confusion because his name is too feminine."

"That's stupid," Chip said. "There are a ton of male celebrities with female or unisex names."

"Yeah? Give me some examples."

"Jamie, Morgan, Taylor, Peyton, Tracy, Sidney...for fuck's sake, Luca. The list goes on and on. Chyna shouldn't cave to this needless pressure. Remember how resistant he was to a switch after he was outed?"

Luca groaned. "Dude, I was there."

"Who's the idiot that turned this into an issue?"

"I think it's a combination of different people and incidents."

"Do Clark and Jody know?"

"Not yet. Chyna's trying to decide on a name before he runs it by the 'rents."

"Okay," Chip said, drawing out the word. "This is newsworthy but not commensurate to all the missed calls and texts. What's the big emergency?"

"Just me wanting to talk to my best friend."

"Aww…I miss you, too. What's going on?"

"I quit football."

"Wait—what? Why'd you do that?"

"I'm overwhelmed by my schedule," Luca admitted. "Besides, I've lost interest."

"I'd understand if that were the truth."

"Why would I lie about something so important?"

Chip's silence was telling.

"Hey, are you still there?"

Clearing his throat, Chip asked, "Are you sure this isn't about Chyna?"

"We hardly have time together," Luca explained. "Throw in football and we might as well break up."

"You know that'll never happen," Chip countered.

"It could," Luca insisted. "You have no idea what goes on in the modeling world. It's one temptation after another."

"And what? You're doubting him already?"

"No, hell no, but I want to be around as often as possible in case he needs me. Anyway, it's a done deal. My dads have given the thumbs-up, so I'm free to enjoy my weekends in Manhattan."

"Luca, you need to chill. Without trust, you guys will break up regardless of your schedule."

Luca sighed.

"You can't insulate Chyna forever," Chip continued in a kinder tone. "Believe me, I tried. My brother has the necessary tools to make good decisions, and you have to remember there's such a thing as overkill. You don't want to end up pushing him away by being overbearing."

"I'm not," Luca protested. "At least I don't think I am."

"Your irrational need to insulate Chyna is coming off as controlling."

"I'll try to hold back my need to lock him up and throw away the key," Luca snarled. "I thought you'd be happy that I'd be around more often."

"Luca," Chip soothed. "You're not doing anything you haven't done in the past, but things are different now. I wouldn't let old fears cloud your judgment, or you might as well move back home. It's time to leave your babysitting days behind."

"What if someone takes advantage of his innocence?" Luca asked. "He's too new at this gig to weed out the creeps from the good guys."

"As usual, you're overthinking. Unless you're planning to be around 24/7, there's nothing you can do from Ithaca to prevent this from happening. Meanwhile, you've given up a sport you've enjoyed since middle school. That's beyond lame."

"You're harder on me than my own dads."

"That's because I know all your dirty secrets," Chip remarked.

"What secrets? I'm an open book."

"You like to be in charge," Chip said. "That's why you were the quarterback. Letting Chyna freefall is so beyond your comfort zone it's making you crazy."

"Shit, yeah," Luca admitted with a frustrated sigh. "What should I do, Chip? Is there a magic pill for my disease?"

"Work on it," Chip said kindly. "I know your intentions are good, and the vigilance was much appreciated when Chyna was going through so much turmoil, but it's got to stop. Talk to him whenever you're feeling uncomfortable about a given situation. Keeping the lines of communication is a must. This way you can voice your concerns without resorting to dumb moves like quitting football."

"Will you give my sport a rest already?"

"You should reconsider," Chip advised. "Football is a great outlet for letting off steam. A winning season will up your confidence and get rid of these unwarranted fears."

"I doubt my coach will let me back on the team. He was pretty pissed when I quit."

"You won't know unless you ask. Enough about you," Chip said. "Is Chyna available?"

"He might still be sleeping."

"Will you go and check?"

When Luca opened the bedroom door, Chyna was sitting up and scrolling through his phone.

"Hey," he said, taking his attention off the screen and smiling. "Where have you been?"

"Chip's on the phone," Luca said, handing it over.

A wide smile followed an outstretched hand. "How was the AT?" Chyna asked excitedly.

"Intense but amazing," Chip remarked. "I broke my phone on the hike, so that's why I've been incommunicado. What's all this about a new name?"

"Do you approve?" Chyna asked.

"Truth?"

"Of course."

"I'm not sure I like the idea. You hated Chandler when we suggested a change."

"Seriously, Chip? Who in their right mind would name a kid Chandler?"

"Dad."

Chyna cackled. "If I change my name, it'll be something a lot more interesting."

"Don't succumb to pressure, kiddo. Make the change if you can't live with Chyna anymore, but if that's not the case, tell the haters to fuck off."

"It's not set in stone yet."

"Good to know," Chip said, sounding relieved. "After all this time, I'm used to Chyna. Imagining you as anything else is going to be a stretch."

"I kind of like Flynn."

"Nope."

"Do you have a suggestion?"

"How about *Precious*?" Chip asked in Gollum's creepy voice.

"Don't be a jerk," Chyna said. "I'm asking for your help. Play the name game with me."

"I don't have time for this."

"Hey! You need to make the time after disappearing for ages."

"What about Phoenix?"

"Why that in particular?"

"It's the Greek mythological bird that is cyclically regenerated or reborn. Sort of like you."

"Hmm."

"Think about it," Chip suggested. "Or you could simply call yourself by your surname, like they do in sports or the military. Davidson should be manly enough for you."

Chyna huffed. "This isn't about me, Chip."

"Gotcha," Chip pounced. "You're giving in to gender bias."

"I suppose I am."

"Don't."

"You're not the one who has to deal with the perplexed looks when I walk through the door."

"Has it occurred to you that they may be stunned by your beauty and not your name?"

"Way to compliment and smack down at the same time."

"Food for thought, bro. There's no need to rush into anything."

"I'll think about it," Chyna said. "Want to talk to Luca?"

"Yeah."

Luca got on the phone, and Chip remarked. "He's determined to do this."

"Seems like it," Luca acknowledged.

"Keep me posted."

"I will. Thanks for finally returning my calls."

"Dude, my phone was dead."

"Heard you the first time," Luca teased. "Don't let it happen again."

"It's not like I can do a hell of a lot from Illinois," Chip complained.

"You're my lifeline, buddy. Talking to you is the next best thing."

"That works both ways. Stay in touch, yeah?"

"Will do," Luca said, disconnecting the call.

Chapter Thirteen

ALEX HAD ACCOMPANIED Zeb on a tour of the 911 Memorial while Luca and I dozed on and off all afternoon. Eventually, the need to get out of the apartment to enjoy a Saturday night together became imperative. My rash was practically gone, so instead of taking another pill, I downed two cups of coffee to wake up. The Benadryl would have to wait until we got home tonight.

Since most of us were underage, Alex suggested Webster Hall in the East Village, which was a club that catered to nineteen and over. I was surprised to see so many familiar faces at the club—models, photogs, and their trusted minions—rushing over to greet me with enthusiastic hugs and air kisses. On the surface, it couldn't be friendlier, but I hadn't been around long enough to tell the phonies apart from the genuine admirers. They sized up my outfit—skinny black jeans and a cropped top—and checked out my companions to see if they were celebrities. Alex was well known, having graced several magazine covers already, and greeted a few friends but didn't leave our side.

The surreptitious glances and cliquey clusters reminded me of high school, only this time the ante was much higher. Fame and fortune were at stake, and hanging out with people who could make or break a career was an art form in and of itself. It took time to cultivate connections, and more often than not, the ruthless pursuit of one's career led to conniving and left little room for true friendship. I was one of the newer faces in town and hadn't proven myself yet. Perhaps next year, or even in six months, I'd be considered an A-lister, but for now, I was another aspiring model trying to get ahead. It would take a lot more than the right name or clothes to become a part of the "in" crowd.

Still, I wasn't invisible, and the sycophants hanging around the scene hit on my companions and me with one goal in mind—sex. Who you slept with was as important as who negotiated your contract. The gushing and playful flirting could knock down self-imposed barriers, and it was easy to fall into the bed-hopping trap.

If nothing else, my past had taught me to be wary of overt signs of friendship. The need to be accepted, carried over from my cheerleading days, had diminished considerably, but like an old wound that ached when prodded, it didn't take much to revert back to the insecure teenager.

An aggressive blond with an impish grin flung himself at Luca and asked for a dance. Pushing the interloper aside, I inserted myself in the vacant spot and snaked my arms around Luca's waist possessively.

"I was going to tell him to back off," Luca said, bemused.

"Saved you the trouble."

"Now he's giving us the stink eye while he chats up your friends."

"Those people aren't my friends," I pointed out. "They're competition."

"Isn't there one person in that group who might actually give a shit about you?"

I glanced over at the crowd of beautiful people and noticed that Ian Carmichael had joined the group and was checking us out. The blond I'd pushed away was whispering in Ian's ear, probably reporting back on my territorial hold on Luca.

"None that I can see," I replied.

"That's sad," Luca whispered close to my ear. My skin rippled with pleasure, and I moved closer, loving the sensation of Luca's hard body pressed against mine.

"Why do this to yourself?" Luca continued. "There's a spot ready and waiting for you at Cornell. You'd be making lasting friendships while earning your degree. Granted, it won't be glamorous, and money will be going out instead of coming in, but it's real. How long do you think this make-believe world is going to last?"

I pressed my forehead against Luca's. "Sometimes, I'm not sure why I'm here. When you're in town and I'm holding you close, all the reasons that made sense at fifteen no longer apply. You're not the only one with jealousy issues. I think of all the hot guys on campus flirting with you. Ugh. I can't even."

Luca cupped my ass and squeezed possessively. "Why in the fuck are we doing this to ourselves?"

"It's not you, Luca. I'm the one with this compulsive need to prove I'm as good, if not better, than anyone out there."

"You can do that in college," Luca said gently. "You don't need to prove anything to me. I've known how special you are for a long time."

Someone tugged at my elbow and I flinched. Ian was looking at me hopefully. "Mind if I butt in?"

"I'm busy...."

"Dude," Luca said. "He's with me."

"I haven't seen Chyna in a while," Ian persisted. "It's only a dance, buddy."

Luca frowned and looked at me for guidance.

"Ian's the photographer I worked with when I first got into town," I explained.

"Right," Luca said, glaring at Ian. "I remember now."

"One dance?" Ian pleaded.

"I'll be back as soon as the song ends," Luca said.

"Who was that?" Ian asked when Luca stormed off. He leaned in so we could hear each other over the pounding beat.

"My boyfriend."

"He's deliciously territorial," Ian said.

"I know."

"Does he model?"

"No. He's studying to be an architect."

"I could make him a superstar if he'd agree to a photo shoot," Ian said. "Talk to him."

"Is that why you asked me to dance? To get to Luca?"

"Among other things," Ian said. "How've you been?"

"Fine."

"I heard you had a reaction to waxing."

"Why is my allergy big news?"

"Your name is starting to crop up more and more," Ian explained.

"Yeah? Has there been any confusion with my name?"

"I don't understand," Ian said, moving closer. "Say that again?"

"Do you think I should change my name to something more masculine?"

Ian cocked his head. "Like what?"

"Phoenix."

"Let's find a quiet corner and discuss this properly," Ian suggested.

I looked around and couldn't see Luca to let him know what was happening. Zeb and Alex were on the other side of the room. Reluctant to appear indecisive, I followed Ian off the dance floor to a table for two that had been recently vacated. Hailing a passing waiter, Ian ordered a beer for himself and a glass of mineral water with a lemon wedge for me.

Once that was out of the way, Ian asked, "What were you saying about your name?"

I explained, and Ian surprised me by vetoing the idea.

"But you specifically asked me about my name the day we met," I pointed out. "You should be in favor of a switch."

"I remember that day," Ian said amused. "You were ready to walk out the door, and I admired you for standing up to me. Your name is unusual for a guy, and yeah, a name change might make life easier all around, but in this business, there's a thing called panache."

"I'm not sure what it means?"

"It means you've got game, kiddo. Phoenix is okay, but Chyna stands out, raises eyebrows, makes you sit up and pay attention."

"Seriously?"

"Absolutely," Ian stated. "You think Madonna didn't get shit for showing up with that ridiculous name? She's the absolute antithesis of the Virgin Mary, but that's what made people look twice. It helped that she was a kick-ass artist and could sway a crowd like no other. Some names are meant to be changed and others stick. You're already making an impact as Chyna. Why fuck with a good thing?"

"Now I'm totally confused," I admitted.

Ian put his arm around me and leaned closer. "Trust me on this one thing, kiddo. I know what I'm talking about."

Before I could reply, Ian was hauled out of his seat, and the murderous look on Luca's face prompted me to stand directly in front of Ian.

"It's not what you think," I explained. "We were talking."

"Looked like something else to me." Luca scowled. "Why aren't you on the dance floor?"

"I wanted advice and we couldn't hear each other."

"On what?"

"My possible name change."

"Now it's a possibility again?" Luca asked incredulously. "Christ, I can't keep up."

Ian straightened out his collar, which had been distorted by Luca's manhandling. He looked ready to retaliate, and Luca got into a fighting stance, but Ian apologized instead of striking a blow.

"I'm sorry if it looked like I was coming on to Chyna," he said, "but I promise you we were only brainstorming. I've been in this business a long time, and I'm hoping my words of advice haven't fallen on deaf ears.

Chyna needs to retain his name to stand out amongst the hundreds who show up in Manhattan on a daily basis. Why be a caterpillar when you can be a butterfly?"

"Those were my original thoughts," Luca said slowly, "but Melinda said otherwise."

"I get that Melinda's his agent and trust has been established, except she isn't me," Ian maintained. "At the risk of sounding like an arrogant bastard, I'm a lot more famous than she is, and if anyone has the right answers about models and what makes them shine, it's me."

"So you're advocating Chyna keep the name?"

"Absolutely," Ian said. "He'd be a fool to mess with a good thing."

"What about all the recent confusion?" Luca asked. "Isn't that something major that needs to be addressed?"

Ian waved away Luca's question like it was a pesky fly. "That's not going to be a problem much longer. Once the word gets around that I'm endorsing your boyfriend, I can promise you no one will wonder who the fuck Chyna is."

Luca looked at Chyna. "What do you think?"

I shrugged, feeling sheepish. "It would save me a lot of trouble."

"And my sanity," Luca admitted. He turned to Ian. "Sorry for being such an ass."

Ian snorted. "It's not the first time I've been accused of something I haven't done."

"Still...I shouldn't have jumped to conclusions."

"How old are you, kid?" Ian asked.

"Nineteen," Luca said. "We both are."

"It's a hell of an age," Ian said derisively. "Not quite legal, but a long distance from childhood. Hormones are more likely to rule than common sense. I don't envy you."

Luca's mouth twisted. "That's what old people say all the time. You'd probably sell your left nut to be twenty again."

Ian barked out a laugh. "Twenty-nine might be preferable."

"Is this entire industry fake?" Luca asked bluntly.

I was shocked by his rudeness but felt marginally better by Ian's reaction.

"That's a million-dollar question," Ian said, smiling. "The very essence of this industry is illusion. There are a few genuine personalities, but the majority are creations of advertising. We photographers perpetuate the fantasy by turning the plain Janes and Joes into elusive gods. At the end of the day, though, when the eye shadow, lipstick, and foundation are washed off, you end up with the ordinary, which accounts for the insecurity and fear—"

"That turns a normally nice person into a raving bitch," I finished.

"Something like that," Ian said. "If you stick around long enough, you'll figure out who's legit and who should be avoided."

Luca reached out to shake Ian's hand, and the photographer met him halfway. "Thank you for your time and advice," he said, sounding genuinely contrite. "I'm sorry for doubting you."

"No worries. Are you sure I can't turn you into a model?"

Luca smiled. "Thanks, but no. One model in our family is more than enough."

"Have you two been together long?" Ian asked.

"Yes," Luca replied.

"Try not to let the bullshit get you down. It's all part of the game, and things will sort themselves out by the end of the first year."

"Is it worth it?" I asked. "I'm starting to wonder."

"I guess it depends on your priorities, kid. If it's money and a gazillion Twitter followers, then you've come to the right place."

"And if that's not it?" I pressed.

"There's no point in sticking around if you're not in this for the right reasons."

I reached for Luca's hand. "I think I've heard enough for now."

Ian shrugged. "I'm not always correct, but I know our industry better than most."

"I'm sure," I agreed. "Thank you, Ian."

"I hope to see you back in my studio soon."

"Call Melinda and she'll set it up."

"Will do."

Luca guided me through the crowd, and we headed to the spot where Alex and Zeb had been line dancing. This time, Alex's arms were wrapped around Zeb's waist, and the shorter man had his face pressed to Alex's chest.

"Whoa," I whispered. "I never saw that coming."

"Me neither," Luca admitted. "I thought Zeb was straight."

"Alex said he wasn't in the market for a boyfriend."

"We suck at this best friend thing," Luca said. "What just happened?"

"Hell if I know," I murmured. "Let's break them apart and head home."

Chapter Fourteen

ON THE RIDE home, Luca kept stealing glances at Alex and Zeb. Not that their sudden pairing was any of his business, but a heads-up would have been nice. If Zeb was gay, there was no reason to keep that bit of information to himself. Then again, maybe this attraction had come as a total surprise to both of them. They were glued together with Alex's arm resting protectively on Zeb's shoulder. When he finally caught his roomie's eye, Luca lifted a querying eyebrow and got a sheepish grin and a shrug in return. Interesting. He'd pry it out of Zeb once they got back to Cornell.

It was close to three in the morning by the time the subway pulled into their stop, not a great time to be walking along the streets of New York, but it was a safe neighborhood so they didn't rush. In the distance, Luca caught sight of a hooded figure pushing a grocery cart down the sidewalk.

"Is that the same guy you gave money to the other night?" he asked Chyna.

Pausing, Chyna peered in the direction of Luca's gaze. He could make out a figure, but the scavenger was between street lamps that were far apart, so he was standing in shadows. Nonetheless, the cart heaped with cans and bottles was familiar.

"I think so."

"He's heading our way," Luca said.

"The poor guy must be freezing."

"Don't make it your problem," Luca advised. "If you hand him another bill, this will turn into a routine."

"Luca's right," Alex interjected. "I know you feel sorry for him but...."

"Why don't you and Zeb go upstairs," Chyna suggested. "We'll take it from here."

"Are you sure?"

"Absolutely," Luca interjected. "You guys must have something better to do than stand around watching us."

Zeb smiled sheepishly. "About the club—"

"You can tell me later," Luca assured him. "Go."

Luca sprinted to catch up to Chyna who was already reaching into his pocket. "Isn't it kind of late to be out and about?" Chyna asked the man.

"There's no set time to rummage through trashcans," the stranger muttered. "What about you? Shouldn't you be home in bed?"

"We've been clubbing."

"Must be nice."

Luca nudged Chyna. "Let's get out of here."

"Wait." Chyna handed over the twenty. "Here you go, buddy. Try to get something warm to eat."

The stranger snatched the bill. "Appreciate the concern. Now listen to your boyfriend and go home."

"How do you know he's my boyfriend?"

The man made a derisive sound and added, "He acts like he owns you."

"What the hell," Luca said, stepping closer. "You don't know shit about me. I'm protecting him from the likes of you. Stay away from here, or I'll call the cops."

"Luca," Chyna protested. "He's not hurting anyone."

"Yeah, fuck off," the stranger growled from inside the folds of his jacket.

"Okay, that's enough," Chyna said. "Lose the attitude and get going, mister."

With his head still bowed, the stranger challenged, "Can't you tell a guy and a girl apart?"

"Sorry," Chyna blustered. "I didn't realize."

"Pay more attention next time."

"Wait," Chyna said, trying to hold the stranger in place. "You're a woman?"

"Get away from me," the muffled voice croaked, rapidly moving in the other direction.

"Hold on," Luca called out.

The retreating figure never stopped, pushing the wobbly cart as fast as possible until she disappeared around the corner.

Head shaking, Chyna called out in a soft voice, "Luca?"

"Yeah, babe?"

"I have this awful feeling in my gut," he replied, clutching Luca's arms for support. "Can we try to find her?"

"Why?" Luca said.

Chyna's brows drew together. "It shouldn't take more than a few minutes."

"What is it with you and that person?"

"I'm not sure," Chyna said, looking confused. "But something's compelling me to find out."

Luca let out an exasperated sigh.

"What if it's Lisa?"

Luca narrowed his eyes. "No. Fucking. Way."

"She obviously knows us," Chyna argued.

"You're letting your emotions get the better of you," Luca said. "There's no way that homeless person is your mother."

"I'm not so sure," Chyna said pensively. "I've felt this strange connection from the first time I laid eyes on her."

"You've always had a soft spot for the underdog," Luca said gently.

"Perhaps, but it's more in this case," Chyna muttered. "We have no idea what happened to Mom after she disappeared. She could be dead, for all I know, but what if she followed me to New York?"

"Wouldn't she have knocked on your damned door if that was the case?"

"We didn't exactly part on good terms," Chyna reminded him.

"Let's discuss this upstairs," Luca said. "It's freezing and that person is long gone. We'll look for her tomorrow if you can't let this go."

"Thank you," Chyna said, hooking his arm under Luca's.

In the apartment, they found Alex and Zeb in the kitchen, sharing cookies and hot chocolate. "Everything okay?" Alex asked.

"Not really," Chyna said, slumping down on a chair.

"Let me get you something warm to drink," Alex said. "Then you can tell us what's going on."

"Sounds wonderful," Chyna said. "Thank you."

After Alex made another pot of hot chocolate and plated more of his famous cookies, they sat around the kitchen table and Chyna got them up to date. Parts of his story had already been shared the night he and Alex had their heart-to-heart, but Chyna had left out the details of his mother's slow descent into madness.

"So let me get this straight," Alex said after listening to the incredible chain of events. "Your mother disappeared the night of your freshman prom?"

"That's right," Chyna said. "We'd uncovered her scheme to keep the school authorities in the dark regarding our immunization records. She knew she'd broken a few laws, on top of shattering our trust as well as jeopardizing our health. Unwilling to face the repercussions, she left without a trace, and Chip and I ended up in foster care."

"What about your dad?" Alex asked.

Chyna shook his head.

"Is he dead?" Zeb asked.

Chyna grimaced. "He may as well be."

"Chyna's dad has taken avoidance to a whole new level," Luca responded. "He wanted nothing to do with the aftermath of Lisa's decision, which sucked because he had the opportunity to stop her at the beginning. None of this would have happened if he'd only listened to the doctor's advice when the twins were born."

Luca put his arm over Chyna's shoulder when he saw him wince.

"I didn't mean to upset you."

"I'm fine," Chyna assured him.

"It's a wonder you're not in rehab or worse," Zeb remarked.

"I was pretty messed up for a while," Chyna admitted. "Having Chip and Luca love me unconditionally kept me grounded. When your own mother—the one person you should be able to trust—has repeatedly lied and molded the truth to suit her purposes—"

"—and your dipshit father didn't take control of the situation—" Luca added.

"—you end up with a massive problem that took time and money to unravel," Chyna finished.

"That's why you've got a chick's name," Zeb concluded.

"Yes," Chyna said. "My dad wanted to name me Chandler, but my mom threw a fit, and she won the battle. Don't get me wrong, I love my name, but it was meant for the female they were expecting, not the male they got."

"No wonder you've been talking about making a change," Zeb stated.

"After discussing it with Ian, I've decided to keep my name."

"Is he the guy you were dancing with at the club?" Zeb asked.

"Yes. Ian's been in the industry a long time and said there was no need to change."

"Let's get back to the problem at hand," Luca broke in. "I think we should call Jody or Clark and let them know what's going on."

"Not until we have the truth," Chyna argued.

"We can't keep patrolling the streets like a bunch of vigilantes," Luca reasoned. "And what do we do when we find her?"

Chyna's expression hardened. "We call the cops."

"Being homeless isn't a crime," Luca reminded him.

"But following me to New York is stalking."

"Do you have any type of restraining order?" Alex interjected. "If so, then the cops will act on that if legal boundaries have been crossed."

"I'm almost sure Jody and Clark filed something to protect us, but I'll have to confirm with Chip."

"Let's do that before you drag the law into the mix," Alex recommended.

"You're assuming the worst?" Zeb asked.

Chyna shrugged. "She's unpredictable."

"New York's a long way from Illinois," Zeb pointed out.

"My mother may be crazy, but she's always been resourceful."

"Lunatics usually are," Alex stated.

The next morning, Chyna called Chip to let him know what had transpired. "Dammit," he muttered after hearing the whole story. "I had a feeling she'd surface at some point."

"What should I do if it turns out to be her?" Chyna asked.

"Call the cops."

"That was my original thought, but what if she just wants to talk?"

"Doesn't matter," Chip said tersely. "I don't want her anywhere near you. Jody filed an Order of Protection with a stay away clause shortly after Lisa abandoned us. He was worried she might change her mind and resurface. Although, come to think of it, the OP ended when we turned eighteen."

"But if she was out of state, there's every chance she wasn't aware it existed," Chyna argued. "A lot has happened since then. If this person is actually Mom, I'd like to find out where she's been all this time. Why is she living on the streets? Aren't you the least bit curious?"

"Not at all," Chip replied. "Lisa is psychotic and being around her isn't a good idea."

"All I want are answers," Chyna said. "What harm can that do?"

"You know Lisa is a manipulative sicko. She shouldn't be given the opportunity to mess with your head now that you've achieved some semblance of normalcy."

"Why aren't you calling her Mom anymore?"

"She lost that privilege when she walked out of our lives."

"Which accounts for our abandonment issues," Chyna muttered.

"Speak for yourself," Chip said. "Months of therapy helped me come to terms with all of mine."

"Lucky you."

"Stay away from her," Chip warned. "Don't expect any answers from that crazy bitch."

"Okay, that's enough hate for one day," Chyna said tiredly. "How's Meghan?"

"She's great," Chip said. "Can I talk to Luca, please?"

"Sure," Chyna replied, handing back the phone.

"Wassup?" Luca asked, walking out of the room.

"Now I'm having a meltdown," Chip admitted.

"Join the club."

"Seriously, dude. Before you go back to school, sit Alex down and make sure he understands they're not dealing with someone rational."

"I'll make sure."

"You think he's strong enough to protect Chyna in case?"

"Yes."

Chapter Fifteen

THE MORNING STARTED out on a promising note when Luca woke to the sweet sensation of Chyna's lips wrapped around his cock. His lover's hair fell in wild waves, grazing Luca's chest, stomach, and thighs like angel wings. Moaning in appreciation, he carded the silky strands, and embraced the moment as Chyna continued to pleasure him. Twisting around to reciprocate, they sucked each other off lazily, taking the time to draw out the loving. There were no subways to catch or classes to attend today, and that alone was cause for celebration.

Later, they feasted on Alex's Southern-style breakfast: biscuits with sausage gravy, country fried steak and eggs, and a short stack of buttermilk pancakes.

"I'd marry you if I wasn't already taken." Luca complimented Alex in between satisfied bites. "You're in the wrong business, buddy."

"Thank you, sugar. I enjoy cooking for friends and relatives, but I'd rather not spend my entire life bent over a hot stove."

"Too bad," Luca said. "I'll be a steady customer if you ever change your mind."

Zeb voiced his desire to continue their tour of the city, and, once more, Alex agreed to be his guide. Which left Luca and Chyna to entertain themselves. As the day progressed, Chyna grew more and more restless. Luca knew it had to do with approaching nightfall. Chyna had insisted they patrol the streets again to try to find the cart-pusher. Alex and Zeb promised to be home by nine so they could cover more territory.

By eight thirty, Chyna was a wreck. Imagining worst-case scenarios had made him more and more agitated as the day progressed. He was wrapping a scarf around his neck when the guys walked through the front door, and he didn't waste time on pleasantries.

"Can we get going?"

Alex paused, taking in Chyna's demeanor. "Are you okay, sugar?"

"I want to get this over with."

"We're ready," Zeb volunteered. "Alex and I had dinner about an hour ago."

"Good," Chyna said. "Let's go."

They found her almost immediately, crouching by a dumpster in a dark alley. Luca didn't want to think about what she must have been doing before their group showed up. He looked at Chyna to see if he'd make a move, but he seemed paralyzed with fear.

"Hey!" Luca called while walking into the alley purposefully. "Can we talk?"

The woman didn't respond, watching him warily as he approached.

"Don't come closer," she warned when he was a few feet away.

Luca slowed. "Relax. We only want to ask you some questions."

"Get the hell out of here."

When he was close enough, Luca yanked the hoodie down to get a better look. He hadn't seen Lisa Davidson in almost four years, and although this person was clearly female, she was nothing like the person he remembered. Living rough had ravaged her complexion, and strands of matted brown hair peppered with gray framed a weather-worn face. She wore layers of filthy clothing, and judging by the sour odor, hadn't been touched by soap in ages. If this was Chyna's mother, she'd most certainly fallen on hard times.

"Mama?" Chyna asked tentatively. "Is it really you?"

"Leave me alone," Lisa murmured, pulling the hood over her head and retreating into the folds.

"It's me," Chyna persisted. "Won't you please talk to me?"

Luca held Chyna back, stepping in between the two of them protectively. "What in the hell are you doing here, Lisa?"

Baring her teeth, Lisa growled, "Stay away."

"You shouldn't be here," Luca said.

"Says who?" she asked, hawking up a loogie and sending it sailing toward Luca's shoes.

He stepped back, looking at her in disgust. "There's a legal document that forbids you from getting too close to Chyna."

Lisa glared. "Why don't you take your righteous anger and leave me the fuck alone."

Luca reached for Chyna's hand. "Let's go, babe. She's obviously not in her right mind."

Lisa bellowed and crashed into Luca, bringing him to his knees. Chyna was by his side in seconds and spitting mad.

"You bitch! Why'd you hurt him?"

"He's a bad influence," Lisa snarled. "Look at you! Acting like a man instead of the young lady I raised."

"You're fucking nuts," Chyna said, helping Luca to his feet.

Infuriated by Chyna's rebuke, Lisa lost it and attacked. Luca dodged, but not fast enough. She got one solid swipe down his neck, scratching him with ragged nails that had turned into lethal weapons. Four lines materialized, dotted with drops of blood. Alex sprinted forward and grabbed Lisa, pulling her away before she could do any more damage. His arms were around her like a vise, keeping her in place despite her furious efforts to get free. She was kicking and flailing and spewing a torrent of hate.

"Call 911," Alex said loudly. "Now!"

Zeb did as instructed, and when that was done, he began to film the scene.

Lisa was still wriggling in Alex's arms and using cuss words that would have put truckers to shame.

The cops arrived and handcuffed Lisa. They put her in the back of the squad car while going over the particulars.

After getting the gist of the altercation, the lead officer began questioning Luca. "Do you know your assailant?"

"She's my mother," Chyna interjected. "What's going to happen to her?"

"We'll have to assess her condition before any decisions are made. How old are you?" the cop asked Chyna.

"Nineteen," Chyna replied. "What's that got to do with anything?"

"I'm gathering information," the cop said. Turning to Luca, he asked, "How about you, sir?"

"Same."

"Looks like you're bleeding."

"That crazy bitch scratched the hell out of me," Luca said.

"You should get it looked at. They may want to give you a couple of shots to prevent any complications."

"Is that necessary?" Luca turned his head and caught Lisa glaring at him malevolently. From a distance, she looked feral, with her lips curled back into a sneer revealing one missing tooth. Whatever decency she'd possessed had long since gone. Turning back to the cop, Luca nodded. "I think I will see a doctor. There's no telling what kind of bugs live underneath that woman's fingernails."

"We can call the paramedics," the cop suggested.

"No, that's okay," Luca said. "We'll go to the emergency room on our own."

"Suit yourself. Before I go, let's replay the incident one more time."

Chyna and Luca took turns explaining.

"And you're certain this woman is your mother?"

"Sadly, yes," Chyna replied. "I can give you my foster father's phone number, and he'll confirm my statement."

"That'll be great."

Chyna rattled off the necessary information, and the cop filled his notepad.

"Actually, I'll need everyone's contact numbers," the cop stated and then looked at Chyna. "Let's start with you."

When he was done, he handed Chyna his card.

"Take this in case you need to get in touch." Addressing Luca, he asked, "Would you like me to call for a ride before we go?"

"Yes, please," Luca replied.

Zeb and Alex's offer to accompany them to the hospital was declined. God only knew how long they'd end up waiting, and there was no point in everyone being miserable. The police stayed until the Uber arrived shortly after.

SHAKEN BY THE altercation with Lisa, I withdrew, choosing to remain silent during the short ride to the hospital. There was nothing I could say to make this situation right. I hoped Luca would take Lisa's mental state into consideration and not press charges. Not that she didn't deserve it, but the woman was seriously in need of help. Thinking about Lisa in the abstract had been a lot less disturbing than seeing her madness manifest in such a horrid way.

Luca tried to draw me out, downplaying his injuries, but my guts were churning. I knew he was lying. The blood on his shirt was a shocking reminder of my mistake. If I hadn't insisted on going after Lisa, none of this would have happened. I should have listened to Chip and kept my distance, but self-reproach was messing with my good sense. If I'd shown more concern back when she first left—rather than relief—and begged the adults in my life to try a little harder to locate her, Lisa might have received the medical attention she deserved.

Reluctant to call Jody and Clark until I got my emotions under control, I watched Luca get treated. They cleaned the scratches, covering them with a light bandage, and followed up with a tetanus booster and a loading dose of penicillin. I was relieved the doctors were doing their best to make sure Luca's wounds didn't get infected, but it also reminded me that Lisa was a bacterial cesspool given her living conditions. How long had it been since she'd had a bath or change of clothes? What did she eat? Where did she sleep? Did she use sex as a form of currency, and if so, had it been safe? One horrible thought after another wreaked havoc on my conscience. All this time, I'd been living the high life, dealing with modeling contracts involving hundreds of thousands of dollars, while Lisa had been doing who-knows-what for food and shelter.

Hot bile rose up unbidden, and I dashed out of the cubicle, down the hallway, and ducked into the first bathroom I could find to spew the entire contents of my stomach. Tears of regret compounded by wracking spasms made me sink to my knees. My hair got in the way as I hugged the toilet bowl, trying to get rid of old demons that had taken up residence so quickly. Chip hadn't been wrong about Lisa's virulent hold on my fragile psyche.

When there was nothing left to vomit, I crawled over to the sink to try to repair the damage. My eyes were bloodshot, and mascara streaked down my cheeks in runny blue rivulets. With my reddened nose, I looked clownish. Stringy saliva and bits of crud hung on the tips of my hair, where it had fallen in the way of the bilious tidal wave. I turned on the faucet full blast and began to clean up, getting rid of all signs of weakness before returning to Luca. He was on the phone talking to Grier when I got back to the cubicle, explaining in detail what had transpired, and reassuring his father that he was fine. Luca pulled out his insurance card to make sure he had all the right information. He also confirmed that he was carrying the credit card he'd been given him for emergencies, and Grier instructed him to use it to pay his deductible when he was discharged.

While Luca was occupied, I decided now was a good time to get Jody on the phone. He answered on the second ring, and as expected, he sounded professional and ready to attend to my crisis. Thank God he was a doctor. Unfortunately, I didn't do as well. I broke the minute I heard the concern in Jody's voice, blubbering out the details like a five-year-old. Jody did his best to soothe me, but the tears kept on coming, and Jody asked to speak to Luca's attending physician to see if they could give me something to ease my anxiety.

It was close to dawn by the time we walked out the doors of the emergency room. They'd given me five milligrams of Valium, and Luca was carrying a plastic bag with the hospital logo on the outside. In it was a small tube of antibiotic cream and more bandages for his scratches. They'd also given him three days' worth of penicillin, urging him to finish all the pills even if he thought it was unnecessary.

I felt a bit like a zombie by the time we arrived at the apartment. The mild sedative had helped knock the edge off my overpowering urge to curl up in a ball and cry again. I didn't know how long this calm would last, but I planned to ask Jody for another prescription if I didn't recover by tomorrow. I couldn't work when my emotions were all over the place. Any bit of criticism would crush me, and if I had to turn to chemicals to grow a sturdier set of balls, I'd do it.

The first thing I noticed upon entering the apartment was the empty living room. Zeb had slept on the sofa the previous evening, but right then, he was MIA.

"I think our roommates have hooked up."

Luca grunted. "Whatever. I'm too tired to figure it out."

"I know we joked about this, but I'm surprised it's actually happening."

"Me too," Luca said, following me to the bedroom. "I'm guessing this is a new thing for Zeb. He's going to bombard me with questions when we get back to Ithaca."

"You're not upset about it, are you?"

Luca shook his head. "About them hooking up? Not at all. The question of Zeb's orientation is the least of my worries. Can we talk about what happened at the hospital?"

"I'd rather not," I said, shutting the bedroom door.

"You had a major meltdown over someone who attacked me," Luca accused. "Frankly, I'm surprised there's any sympathy left for Lisa after what she did to you."

I didn't respond, and I could tell Luca was getting frustrated.

"Talk to me, Chyna."

"Are you planning on pressing charges?"

"Why shouldn't I? Your mother drew blood! Do you expect me to turn the other cheek? When in hell did I become the bad guy?"

"You heard her," I replied, trying to make sense of my thoughts, which were a little foggy from the Valium. "She thinks you turned me."

"Like I have super powers or something?" Luca retorted. "I had nothing to do with your decision. That was between you and your shrink. Don't you dare lay that on me after I tried my hardest to stay neutral."

"Whatever," I said tiredly. "Lisa thinks I'm incapable of thinking for myself. She had no idea I'd been having second thoughts for weeks leading up to prom, and, yes, I know you did your best to keep your opinions to yourself. I'm not saying Lisa's opinions are legit, but it's what she believes."

Luca sank down on the bed. He'd stripped down to his briefs, and I felt a sharp pang of pity when I saw the bruising around Luca's knees and the bandage on his neck, harsh reminders of Lisa's insanity.

I put my arm around Luca's shoulders and drew him closer. "I'm sorry. I'm not defending her, but she is my mother. The person who hurt you isn't the Lisa I grew up with."

"Shit."

Luca's voice broke at the end, and I knew he regretted his outburst. My mood plummeted, and it made me sadder knowing my own mother had come between us.

I kissed him on the cheek and felt a little better when Luca remarked, "We're both reacting—I know you'd never take her side over mine."

"Do you still love me?"

"Whoa," Luca said. "Don't start. My loving you isn't negotiable."

"I've been nothing but trouble from day one."

"Hey, we've had a lot of ups and downs, but most of the drama in our lives has been created by other people. You and I are solid. I don't want to ever hear you say otherwise."

"I love you." I pulled him down on the mattress. "Let me show you how much I care."

"I can always use a reminder," Luca said.

We fell asleep after lazily sucking each other off, and I woke up around two in the afternoon. Silently, I pulled up flannel lounging pants, threw on a long-sleeved T, and slipped out of the room. Luca would wake up soon enough, but for the moment, sleep was the best cure for his unfortunate run-in with Lisa.

Alex and Zeb were in the kitchen. There was coffee in the pot and a crock pot of something that smelled delicious.

"Good morning," I said, grabbing a mug. "Whatever you're making smells wonderful."

"It's early afternoon, sugar. And what you're smelling is plain old gumbo."

"What's in it?"

"I normally use seafood, but since all we had was chicken, I went with that. Thank goodness we had all the other ingredients in the freezer, so I didn't have to go to the store."

"Is it ready?"

"Yes, do you want some?" Alex asked.

"I'll try it," I said. I looked at Zeb who'd been quietly observing the exchange. "Cat got your tongue?"

Zeb shook his head.

"What then?"

"There's nothing to say," Zeb responded.

"Sorry about my mother's psycho moment," I said. "You guys didn't need to be a part of that."

"It's fine," Alex said. "We have our fair share of crazies in the South. No need to apologize."

"I do have a question," Zeb posed. "Are you determined to keep the name Chyna?"

I took a spoonful of the gumbo and sighed with happiness before answering. "It's probably easier all around. Ian convinced me that it was unique and already creating a buzz."

"You told us it was causing confusion," Zeb corrected.

"I might have overreacted."

"Okay," Zeb replied. "Your decision."

I spat out a slice of green into my hand. "What is this?"

"Haven't you ever had okra?" Alex asked.

I made a face. "Tastes like jizz."

Alex's eyes rounded in surprise, and then he burst into laughter.

I turned to Zeb. "Doesn't it?"

"I...wouldn't...don't...are you kidding me?" Zeb flushed. He stood and quickly left the room.

"Oops. Did I out him?"

Alex gave a half smile. "Not really."

"So, wait a sec," I said, leaning forward. "You guys hooked up?"

Alex made a zipping motion across his lips.

Luca walked in and sniffed. "Smells great in here."

"It's just spunk according to your boyfriend," Alex said.

"Shut up," I replied, grinning.

"I'll eat whatever you've cooked," Luca said.

Alex laughed while he filled Luca's bowl with the gumbo.

"You'd better go after Zeb," I suggested to Alex. "I hate to see him suffer longer than necessary."

"What'd I miss?" Luca asked.

"I might have outed Zeb."

Luca's gaze flitted from Alex to me and back to Alex. "Is he gay?"

"Not my story to tell, sugar," Alex said. "Go ahead and enjoy your meal. I'll go and check on Zeb."

"Remind him we have to be at the bus stop by five if we want to get back at a decent time."

"Will do."

Chapter Sixteen

"THAT'S IT FOR now," Alex remarked with a final wave to Zeb and Luca who were on their way back to Cornell. Sighing, he turned to me. "Ready to go?"

I nodded and stuck my hands in my coat pockets. Bacon walked briskly in front of us, stopping every so often to sniff and piddle, a routine I was getting more familiar with now that I shared dog-walking duties.

Alex's solid presence was reassuring, and his ability to withhold judgmental comments was a definite plus. I was more inclined to confide in him than anyone else. After last night's encounter with Lisa, I'd stopped thinking of her as my mother. She was nothing like the person I remembered, and following Chip's lead, I decided to use her given name.

Dealing with follow-up calls from Jody, Clark, and also Chip, who'd been informed of last night's incident, was exhausting. Everyone was generous with advice, but none of them had anything positive to convey. The one person who had a right to be interested—my biological father and Lisa's ex-husband—hadn't bothered to call. Her sudden appearance after disappearing without a trace three years ago should have aroused his curiosity, but true to form, Jack Davidson, the douchebag I called Dad, hadn't even sent a concerned text. I never understood how he could be so heartless, considering Lisa had been his wife for years and mother of two of his four children.

Reluctantly, I admitted that Luca, and the rest of my extended family, had my best interests at heart. Judging by my emotional reaction at the hospital, it was apparent I was still tethered to the woman who'd given me life. Crazy or not, Lisa was my mother, and we'd been close until I hit puberty. If there was anything I could do to help with her recovery—if that was even a possibility—I wanted to try. The first thing to do was call the cop who'd responded to the 911 call. He'd know where they were holding her and what could be expected by way of a hearing and sentence.

Back at the apartment, Alex reheated the gumbo, and we ate in front of the TV with Bacon plopped happily at our feet. Instead of diving into my current problems, which had been front and center the entire weekend, I thought I'd give Alex a chance to talk about Zeb. On the surface, there appeared to be a strong attraction, but I didn't want to assume. I put my empty bowl on the coffee table.

"Do you want to talk about Zeb?"

Alex flashed a toothy smile. "I like him."

"I figured that out on my own."

"The thing is I expected a straight dude, but he's much more complex. We had some seriously good conversations."

"You were pasted to each other on the dance floor," I pointed out.

Alex ducked his head, but not before I saw the flush of embarrassment blooming on his cheeks. It was at once endearing and unexpected. I wanted to hold him in my arms and tell him things would work out, but I didn't know that for sure so I held back. I tried to gather more information, though.

"Tell me more," I prompted.

"We're inexplicably drawn to each other," Alex admitted. "I'm not sure why at this point."

"Chemistry?"

"There's that, of course, but something about Zeb set me at ease from the beginning. He sees me for what I am and likes what he sees."

"So he's bisexual?"

"At the very least."

This time, I didn't hesitate and gave him a big hug. "I'm happy for you, Alex."

"Don't pick out the china yet, sugar. We're at the beginning of our journey."

"Here's hoping it'll be filled with nothing but good things."

Alex beamed and then quickly sobered. "How are you doing? Last night must have been rough on you."

I felt instantly vulnerable but answered truthfully. "It was a shock to see my mother like that. She and I have had our differences and, to be clear, they were major, but when she left, I assumed she'd land on her feet. In her own warped way, she was smart and resourceful. I never expected to find her living on the streets. I can't stand by and do nothing, Alex."

"What about your fathers?"

"I'm not sure they're interested in getting involved, and if I tell them I want to help Lisa, they'll panic."

"Why?"

"They're afraid any contact with her will twist me into knots again."

"What do you think?" Alex asked. "Is your psyche that fragile?"

I shrugged. "Aren't people like us more susceptible?"

"Some of us more than others."

"I'm still working on a few issues."

"Feel free to share," Alex prompted.

"Being intersex is like schizophrenia to a lesser degree. I've been trying to coexist with contradictory or incompatible elements my entire life. Outwardly male while inwardly some female. There's a part of me that will always feel like the missing link between two sexes. Even at my most grounded, I'm not one hundred percent sure of who's in charge."

"Oh, honey, that's awful," Alex exclaimed. "Does Luca know how you feel?"

"Yes and no," I admitted. "Most of the time, I'm fine, especially when we're together. I'm happy with my life and my decision to embrace my male form, but once in a while, something will trigger a reaction, and I start spiraling. My mother is like a mind ninja. She knows which buttons to push to turn me into a head case."

"Then why in the hell do you want to have anything to do with her?"

"I love her," I admitted. "At the moment, I don't like her at all, but despite everything she's done wrong, I can't ignore her while she's so messed up."

Alex's mouth flattened into a grim line. "Do you have a plan?"

"Not yet, but I will after I talk to the cops tomorrow."

"You have my support, sugar, but only if you keep me in the loop. Do this on your own and I'm calling Luca or your dads."

"That's not fair," I argued. "I've confided in you because I trusted you'd be discreet."

"I won't let you down, but leaving you alone with her makes me uncomfortable. Especially after you've admitted Lisa has such a powerful hold."

"I'll do what I have to do so she'll get help."

"Within reason," Alex said.

"What does that mean?"

"I won't know until it happens."

"You're making no sense," I said bitterly.

Alex reached for my hand, and I didn't resist, because I needed a friend right then.

"The situation is far from ideal," Alex stated gently, "but I know love isn't always rational, especially when it comes to family. My job as your bestie is to keep you grounded, as you call it, and to make sure you don't fall down that insecure rabbit hole again."

"Thank you," I said. "When you put it that way, it's less insulting. I'm tired of people telling me what I can or can't do. If I'm strong enough to be on my own in New York City, then doesn't it stand to reason that I'm capable of making good decisions?"

"It never hurts to have a Jiminy Cricket by your side. Granted, I'm the furthest thing from that teeny-tiny bug, but my voice is loud and clear. I'll speak up if something feels off."

"Fair enough," I said. "But please watch what you say when you talk to Zeb. Luca will have a meltdown if he finds out I'm trying to help Lisa."

"I promise," Alex agreed.

"First thing in the morning, I'm going to find out where they're holding her. If I can visit, I will."

"Don't you have work commitments tomorrow?" Alex asked. "I have to be at a photo shoot by ten."

"I don't have anything until Wednesday. We're catching a late flight to Miami for that bathing suit thing. I'll be back on Saturday."

"Be careful if they let you talk to her. She's unbalanced and may take it out on you," Alex worried. "Maybe I can move my schedule around so I can accompany you."

"Don't worry," I assured him. "Cops will be all over the place."

"All right. But text if something goes horribly wrong."

I gave him an incredulous eye roll.

"Just saying, sugar."

I slept in the next morning, and when I walked into the kitchen around ten, there was a full pot of coffee Alex had thoughtfully prepared. After pouring myself a cup, I reached for Officer Matt Fletcher's card.

Naturally, the call went to voice mail, so I left a detailed message. By the time I'd consumed a bowl of cereal and another cup of coffee, my phone rang.

"Hey," I greeted. "Thanks for returning my call."

"Who is this?"

"Chyna Davidson. You answered a 911 call we placed last Saturday night."

"I remember. What can I do for you?"

"Can you tell me where I might find the homeless person you took into custody?"

"You mean your mother?"

"Yes."

"She's in a holding cell at the Tombs, awaiting a hearing."

"Excuse me? Did you say the tombs?"

"Sorry, it's the local term for the Manhattan Detention Complex on White Street."

"Downtown?"

"Around the Civic Center."

"What charges is she facing?"

"Even though your boyfriend isn't pressing charges for the assault, she's committed a couple of Class B misdemeanors that need to be addressed."

"How do you know my boyfriend isn't pressing charges?"

"We spoke to him and his father separately yesterday. They're willing to hold back if your mother agrees to a psych evaluation and treatment."

I was relieved that everyone had arrived at a reasonable—and compassionate—solution. It would have been nice if I'd been informed of the decision, but I counted this as a small win.

"What misdemeanors are you talking about?"

"They fall under the Disorderly Conduct statute: fighting and harassing behavior."

"And what's the punishment?"

"A maximum of fifteen days in jail and a fine. The judge might reduce the sentence if your mother agrees to follow the psychiatrist's recommendations."

"Why wouldn't she?"

"She's mentally disturbed? No disrespect, sir, but I'm not sure she can be persuaded to do the right thing."

"This is why I need to see her."

After giving me directions, he offered to meet me at noon. "I'll be there."

"Okay," Officer Fletcher said, disconnecting.

After washing up, I threw on a long-sleeved T and some acid-washed jeans, pulled my hair into a knot on top of my head, and covered it with a Yankee cap.

Grabbing my leather jacket, I headed for the subway. As instructed, I went directly to the holding station attached to the courthouse. True to his word, Officer Fletcher was at the door. He accompanied me to the waiting room and remained there in case I needed help.

After a few minutes, Lisa walked in with her head lowered. She was wearing the same dirty clothes but at least her hands and face were clean. Mistakenly, I assumed they'd hand her a change of clothing, but maybe they were waiting until the court appearance.

Turning to Officer Fletcher, I asked. "Shouldn't she be wearing some kind of prison clothes?"

"This is a holding station, not Rikers," Fletcher responded. "She'll be given something decent to wear before she goes before the judge."

"I see."

"What do you want?" Lisa asked, gaze darting between Fletcher and me.

"Your son wants to talk to you."

Lisa stared at me. "That's not Chip."

I removed the ball cap and my hair tumbled down. "Take another look."

For an instant, there was a flash of recognition, but then Lisa's demeanor changed, and she snarled. "You're no son of mine."

I sighed. "I'm Chyna, Mama."

She frowned and retreated to the far side of the room where she crouched down, wrapped her arms around her waist, and rocked back and forth.

This was the last thing I expected.

"Fuck." My muttered expletive escaped before I could bite back the word.

"I'm sorry," Officer Fletcher said. "She's in bad shape if she doesn't recognize her own kid."

"It's a long story," I replied. "Without going into a lot of detail, I'd like to find a change of clothing and try again."

"I don't understand."

"Is there any place nearby where I can buy a dress or a skirt?"

Officer Fletcher cocked his head.

"You think I'm as nuts as she is."

"I'm trying to understand what's going through your mind," he said politely.

"Like I said a few minutes ago. It's a long and convoluted story. Can you help me find some clothes?"

"There's nothing around here as far as shopping options go."

"I didn't think so." Frustrated, I asked, "Will you be here much longer?"

"I'm only here at your request."

"Will they let me back in if you're gone?"

"I'll make sure they do. Are you going shopping?"

"Something like that," I murmured.

Chapter Seventeen

I STOOD ON the sidewalk and weighed my options. Changing my overall appearance to some semblance of the person Lisa left behind would take time. Aside from clothing, I'd need shoes and makeup to complete the illusion. There was no guarantee that a do-over would jog her memory. She seemed completely out of it, but I'd kick myself if I didn't try.

Shopping was a tedious process, and I wasn't in the mood to wander up and down the aisles to find the perfect outfit. It would be simpler to borrow something, but Melinda was back in Chicago, and I didn't know anyone else in the industry who might be willing to help without prying.

But that wasn't true. Ian Carmichael had repeatedly offered to guide me through the ins and outs of the modeling world. It was a nice gesture, but I'd been reluctant to reach out in case he expected favors in return. I'd heard often enough that relationships between models and photogs were symbiotic. I wasn't prepared to barter, but right then, I was stuck, and he seemed like the logical choice. He had a room full of outfits he used for his photo shoots, and throwing something together on short notice wouldn't be a problem. He also had drawers full of makeup.

Thankfully, I'd entered him into my contacts list. I brought up his number, and considering my decision one last time, I took a deep breath and put in the call.

Ian met me at the door of his studio and led me straight to the huge walk-in closet. He only asked a few pertinent questions—which elevated him in my eyes—but he did point out that going glam might have the opposite effect. He suggested I keep it simple.

With that in mind, I picked out a navy sweater dress with red trim, a matching pair of red knee-high boots, and a cross-chest purse. I brushed out my hair, letting it fall free, and used the barest amount of makeup. Ian stared at me when I walked out of the room.

"Damn, you make a fine woman."

"Thanks but that ship has sailed."

"Was there ever any doubt?" Ian asked curiously.

"As a matter of fact, there was, but my story will have to wait for another time. Thank you for being so accommodating," I said sincerely. "It means a lot."

"I told you to call whenever," Ian said. "Keep the clothes. You never know when they might come in handy again."

"Do you have a shopping bag or something I can use to carry home my original clothing?"

"Please," Ian said. "I have tons of bags."

He left the room and returned with a Bloomingdale's bag. I shoved my clothes inside, and Ian walked me to the door. The Uber was already waiting when he swung it open. "Good luck, Chyna. I hope it all works out."

I kissed him on the cheek and hurried down the steps of the brownstone. In the cab, I thought of Lisa. Of all the scenarios I'd imagined for my mother, homelessness and possible jail time wasn't one of them.

After her sudden departure on the worst night of my life, I stopped wanting to know where she'd gone. I was too hurt, disillusioned, and angry. The longer she stayed away, the less I cared. Dealing with the aftermath of her delusions—in the most painful and public way—and her continued absence in the days, weeks, and months that followed confirmed what I'd always known. Lisa was a coward and chose escape rather than face the ramifications of her poor choices.

What I'd never considered was a true psychotic break. The family was quick to throw the word crazy around, but why had no one realized she wasn't in her right mind for years? Lisa needed help as soon as Chip and I were born, but nobody had intervened. I ended up collateral damage, and it was only after Jody and Clark took me under their wing that professional help had been brought in to heal my psychological wounds.

Which was the main reason I was sitting in a cab playing dress up. I didn't think Lisa was capable of acknowledging me as her other son. She'd mentally checked out, and there wasn't any point in trying to argue. I would perpetuate her delusion for now and pass myself off as her daughter. This time, however, it was with forethought. There was no mistaking my intentions. I paused for a second, stunned by the revelation that I'd successfully crossed over from confused victim to a more confident young adult. It was so satisfying I wanted to send out a mass email. My family members—biological and adopted—were convinced I'd revert to the gender-confused kid when confronted with Lisa, but that wasn't the case. I'd found my inner strength and rallied. It was exciting and I wanted to let the whole world hear about my success, but it would have to wait. At the moment, my priority was gaining Lisa's trust, or nothing would move in the right direction.

To my surprise, Officer Fletcher had waited for me. More importantly, he didn't say a word when I showed up in a dress. He relieved me of the shopping bag and ushered me back to the visitors' section. When the guards brought Lisa out the second time, she wasn't happy. Hissing and snarling like a trapped cat, she tried to jerk out of the jailer's possessive grip. When she turned her sights on me, I cringed, expecting her to scratch my eyes out. To my surprise, her anger was replaced with confusion.

"Chyna?" she asked plaintively.

"It's me, Mama."

Lisa shuffled closer. "When did you get here?"

"A few minutes ago."

Rushing forward before Officer Fletcher could stop her, Lisa flung her arms around my waist and sobbed. I froze, staring down at her filthy head. She was half a foot shorter, and I got a good look at the matted hair, flecked with dandruff and other debris. I didn't want to think what else might be residing in the knotted mess, but the smell of an unwashed scalp—and body—permeated my nostrils. Guiltily, I put aside my feelings of revulsion and patted her gently on the back.

When the crying subsided, I looked into her bleary eyes. "It's okay." I said. "I'm going to get you some help."

"Where have you been all this time?" Lisa whined. "I've searched and searched and couldn't find you."

The harsh glare from the overhead fluorescent lights accentuated the flaws on Lisa's formerly attractive face. I took in the deep commas bracketing her mouth and the crow's feet. Tiny vertical lines on her upper lip and the missing front tooth aged her by decades.

"I've been right here, Mama."

"But I never saw you," Lisa said, looking confused. "How's the cheerleading going?"

Lisa's brain must have reset back to the days before she walked away. In her messed-up mind, I was fifteen years old and a high school freshman.

"I made the squad," I lied.

Let the doctors deal with her reality. It was my job to make sure she accepted the help I was extending. "We're going to clean you up and get you out of here as soon as possible," I continued. "All you have to do when they bring you in front of the judge tomorrow is agree to follow the rules. We'll do the rest."

"What judge?" Lisa asked. "I'm not a criminal. Why am I here? Is this a jail? Where's Chip? Is he back from school yet? He'll fix this. You can't. Get your brother!"

Questions flew out of her mouth in a whiny crescendo.

I stepped back, suddenly afraid. "You need to calm down."

Lisa lunged and grabbed both my arms. For someone who looked so broken, she was strong, and the pinch of her fingers would probably leave bruises.

"Don't you dare tell me to calm down," she screamed. "There's nothing wrong with me."

The two guards pried her away and dragged her out of the room. Her loud protests resounded even when the door closed, and the only thing left of my visit was a sick feeling in my gut.

"Damn," I muttered, rubbing my arms.

"You were getting through for a while," Officer Fletcher said. "Don't blame yourself."

"Somewhat," I corrected. "She still thinks I'm fifteen and a girl."

"About that," Officer Fletcher said, staring at my outfit. "I'm sure there's a perfectly good explanation...."

"As I said earlier, it's a long story, and I'd rather not get into specifics."

"A one-liner would be helpful in case I'm questioned," he said firmly.

I couldn't understand why it would matter to anyone, but the officer had done me a solid, and I didn't want him to get in trouble. "I'm intersex, and Lisa raised me as a girl by mistake. The last time she saw me I looked like this," I said, pointing at my outfit. "I thought it might help."

Looking sympathetic, Officer Fletcher nodded. "Thank you for sharing."

"You're welcome. Can you tell me what's next for my mother?"

"She'll go before a judge tomorrow. Is anyone going to represent her?"

"Not that I'm aware."

"Would your foster father have some answers?"

"I don't know," I replied. "But I can find out."

"Someone should come and put in a good word or at least confirm Lisa's not in her right mind," Officer Fletcher stated. "Her own lawyer would be ideal, but if she has no one to represent her, they'll assign a public defender."

"I don't know anything about the law," I admitted. "But I'd be willing to be a character witness if that'll help."

"Can't hurt."

"What time is the hearing?"

"They don't give you exact times, only a window. In her case, it'll be between nine and twelve."

"All right. I'll be here."

"Do you want to change back into your clothes?" Officer Fletcher asked, handing me the bag he'd put aside.

"Nah, that's okay. The sooner I leave this depressing place, the better. Will I see you tomorrow?"

"Probably not," Officer Fletcher replied. "The truth is I haven't checked my schedule, but if I'm free, I can pop in and see how you're doing."

"That's great," I said. "If I don't see you tomorrow, I want to thank you for your assistance. I know this went over and above your normal call of duty."

"You're welcome. I hope your mother gets the help she needs."

"That makes two of us," I said grimly.

On the way home, I brooded over my failure. Could I have done anything more to lessen the hostility that sprang forth with so little provocation? I shuddered recalling the sudden shift from befuddled to dangerously unmanageable. Lisa was a menace at this point, to herself as well as others.

What made things even worse was her grimy appearance. It didn't make her a sympathetic character, rather the opposite. At least we'd had a brief moment when she'd appeared happy to see me. Well, not my authentic self, but the daughter she'd left behind. Had I made a mistake posing as a girl?

No, I didn't think so. Clearly, I'd done my best, given the scenario. Tamping down the guilt, I considered my next move. I had to call Jody or Chip for advice, but there was a part of me that resented Jody for omitting the truth. He hadn't informed me that Grier had spoken to the cops yesterday. Jody must have been aware of the call, because the four men—Grier, Lil, Jody and Clark—were inseparable and shared every last detail of their lives.

I had a right to know what was going on, and I wanted to weigh in on any decisions made regarding Lisa. It was insulting to be left in the dark. Most likely, my foster fathers and Chip were wringing their hands, doing their damn best to keep me from actually coming face-to-face with Lisa. Well, fuck that shit.

I pulled out my phone and rang Jody. It went straight to voice mail. So did Clark's phone as well as Chip's. Shit. Where were they? There was no point in calling Luca. He'd flip out, cut class, and take the first bus to Manhattan. I didn't want or need my overprotective boyfriend breathing down my neck.

A soft whistle from the bearded guy across the aisle on the subway made me shift my attention. Dressed all in black, with a tribal tattoo encircling his neck, he was staring at my crotch. Too late, I realized I'd been sitting with my legs slightly apart—like a dude—instead of knees pressed together as I'd done for years in girl fashion. Crossing my legs, I turned sideways, but not before flipping the guy off. The fucker snorted with laughter. Asshole.

Thankfully, he got off one stop before mine. The walk home was unpleasant due to the cold temps and no jacket. Mine was crumpled up in the shopping bag, and I didn't feel like stopping to fish it out. I wanted to get home as soon as possible. I was shaking by the time I turned the key in the lock. Bacon greeted me in his usual fashion, yipping and hopping around in circles. I picked him up and headed straight for the kitchen to make myself a cup of coffee.

Jody, Clark, Chip, and Alex were gathered in the tiny room, and their eyes zeroed in on my attire. The collective gasps of horror would have been comical if I hadn't been so wrung out by the emotional afternoon. An intervention wasn't exactly what I'd planned for the evening.

"What in the hell," Chip muttered.

"My lord," Alex exclaimed.

"Where have you been?" Jody asked, scowling.

"Why are you wearing a dress?" Clark asked, looking confused.

I tensed, forgetting the cold and hunger as they lobbed questions in unfounded anger. These were the men in my life, the people who supposedly loved me.

"Really? You see me in a dress and immediately arrive at the wrong conclusion."

"Why don't you tell us what's going on," Jody said, shifting to a gentler doctor mode.

I glared at him. "Don't treat me like a head case," I threatened. "I went downtown to see Lisa. She didn't recognize me in pants, so I scrounged up this outfit to see if it would help jog her memory."

"I see," Jody said.

Furious, Chip stepped forward and got right in my face. "Why did you go down there when I specifically asked you to stay away from her?"

"Because I fucking felt like it," I spat.

"What did you hope to accomplish?" Jody asked calmly.

"I want her to get help."

"Did she agree?"

I shook my head. "She lost it after a few minutes."

"In what way?" Jody asked.

"Does it matter?" I asked, frustrated. "Is one form of crazy better than another?"

"No," Jody said. "I'm trying to determine her state of mind."

"She's lost," I said. "The little bit of sanity Lisa was clinging to before she took off has vanished. The person I just left stinks like garbage and looks like she's eighty years old. Beyond her shocking appearance is her complete lack of comprehension. Lisa needs our help."

"She doesn't deserve jack shit," Chip said.

"You can ignore her all you want, Chip, but I won't. She's our mother."

"Who abandoned us!"

"Get over it!" I shouted. "Lisa has no idea what's right or wrong. How will you become an effective physician if you can't find it in your heart to forgive?"

Stunned by the unexpected reprimand, Chip stepped back. His eyes, so similar to mine, turned dark blue with unshed tears.

"Chip?" I pleaded. "She needs us now more than ever."

His control slipped, and we fell into each other's arms and cried. For the mother we deserved and didn't get, and the father we had, who didn't want any part of our lives.

Chapter Eighteen

WE WERE SITTING around the kitchen table when I got a text from Luca. He was downstairs wanting in. I stared at the message for a few seconds before I hit the app that unlocked the front door.

"Now what?" I wondered out loud.

"What's the matter?" Jody asked.

"Luca's downstairs."

"Finally," Chip said.

"Let him in," Jody stated.

I frowned. "Why didn't anyone tell me he was coming tonight?"

"Grier and I talked about meeting here," Jody said, "when we spoke about Lisa yesterday."

"Are you saying Grier is downstairs as well?"

"I'm guessing he is," Jody said. "With Lil."

"You guys are lame."

"Why?" came the multiple queries.

Standing, I looked at the clueless faces around the room and lost it. "You've kept me out of the loop, and it's insulting. Stop treating me like I'm five."

"We were trying to make things easier," Jody apologized.

"For me or you?"

Without waiting on his reply, I walked out of the room and headed for the front door. Luca was sandwiched between his two dads, and the trio stared at me like I'd grown a third eye.

Belatedly, I realized I hadn't changed yet. "About the outfit—"

"What the fuck?" Luca demanded.

"It's not what you think," I said, frowning at his reaction.

"Why don't you tell us what we're thinking," Luca said slowly.

My head almost exploded at his condescending tone. I was not going to be *handled*. Clenching my fists, I ordered, "Go back to Ithaca."

"Sweetie, there's no need to be upset," Lil countered diplomatically. "We're here to support you."

I whirled around and headed straight for my room with Luca on my heels.

At the door, I warned Luca. "Get out of here, or I'll kick your ass with my fucking stilettos."

He wouldn't budge. "Let me in so we can talk."

"There's nothing you can say that'll make a difference," I said. "Your knee-jerk reaction to my outfit speaks for itself."

Luca tried shouldering past me, but I pushed him away. For the first time in our relationship, I wanted to smack him upside the head. His next question elevated my blood pressure to dangerous levels.

"Instead of getting pissed, you should explain," Luca demanded. "Why are you wearing a dress?"

I wasn't sure it would be worth the effort. He'd already judged me without getting the facts.

"Well?"

"Don't you *well* me, Luca Dilorio."

"Chyna, you're not making this easy."

"Why should I? You people have obviously decided I'm a mindless bot who can't hold my own when confronted with my mother."

"That's not true," Luca said. "It did cross my mind for a brief second, but then I realized I wasn't giving you enough credit—"

"No shit! You're constantly questioning my decisions."

"Look at you," Luca protested. "One meeting with Lisa and you're dressed like...."

"A Kardashian? This is the best I could do on short notice."

"Why do it at all?"

"IT WAS NECESSARY!"

Luca stepped back. "Please tone it down."

"I'll yell if I want to."

"You'll scare the family."

"Fuck the family! What about my fear, huh? Didn't it occur to any of you that I would have liked some emotional support? I had to go and see where they were holding Mom. The last time I laid eyes on her, she was a deranged stranger in the back of a police car. If you had stayed over last night—or bothered to pick up the phone—a misunderstanding could have been avoided."

Luca sighed and sank down on the bed.

"Come here," he said gently. "Please."

"Give me one good reason why I should."

"When I left you yesterday, I didn't know I'd be back so soon," Luca explained. "My dad called me last night. Evidently, he and Lil flew into La Guardia soon after they spoke to Jody about the incident with Lisa. They had me catch the afternoon bus so I wouldn't miss my morning classes."

"And you didn't think it was important to let me know that the 'rents were on the move? Everyone's been making arbitrary decisions about my mother without any input from me. Is that fair? Doesn't that scream disrespect?"

Luca's face crumpled. "I'm sorry. That still doesn't answer my question, though. Why are you dressed like a girl?"

"Woman."

"What-the-fuck-ever."

"Mom didn't recognize me when I showed up looking like a dude."

"You *are* a dude," Luca corrected.

"And you're acting like an idiot," I rounded. "I had to get her cooperation to the point where she'd listen to reason and agree to a psyche evaluation and treatment. How can I do that if she won't even acknowledge me as her child?"

"Isn't she certifiable, though? We all know she's nuts."

"The judge will need an official report from a psychiatrist. They're not going to take my word for it."

"Jody's a doctor."

"He's not licensed in this state. It has to be someone appointed by the court."

"Why go to court at all if I'm dropping the charges? Did she break any actual law other than attacking me without provocation?"

"Don't remind me."

"Seriously, Chyna. What can they charge her with?"

"There are some misdemeanors that'll generate a fine."

"So this charade was part of your master plan to get Lisa to come to her senses?"

"It was the only thing I could think of. Unfortunately, I didn't succeed."

"What happened?"

"She recognized me for a few minutes, and then she flipped out."

"I think she's way beyond a bait and switch," Luca said. "Lisa might be genuinely certifiable."

"Perhaps, but we won't know unless she's evaluated by a shrink."

"Are you going to dress up again tomorrow?"

"I'll do what's best for her."

"I'm sure that Jody will have a suggestion."

"No doubt," I muttered. "You all have a valid opinion, unlike mine, which counts for nothing."

"That's not true," Luca protested. "Now that I know the motive behind your actions, I'll stand by your decision."

"Mighty big of you," I ranted. "Why can't you accept my decisions at face value? When was the last time you automatically trusted that I'd do the right thing?"

Luca didn't respond.

"You suck at letting go."

"I only want to protect you," he said softly.

"What if I tell you I'm going to cross-dress in public whenever the mood hits."

"For Lisa?"

"For me."

"Is this some kind of test?" Luca asked warily.

"It's an honest question that deserves an honest reply."

"Are you punishing me for doubting you?"

"So you view my cross-dressing as a form of punishment?"

"No, that's not...what I meant," Luca stammered. "I'm trying to understand where this conversation is going."

"Would you be ashamed to be seen with me if I wore a dress in public once in a while?"

"Only if you were questioning your gender again," Luca said, sounding surer of himself. "To my mind, it would be a step back. I don't have issues with cross-dressers in general. It's hot when you go femme under your jeans."

"It must be exhausting worrying about my state of mind all the time," I commented dryly. "You're convinced I'll crash and burn at the slightest provocation. That my female alter-ego will overpower my male like some preternatural creature."

"You sort of lost it at the hospital," Luca explained. "What was I supposed to think?"

"That I had a shock and reacted like any normal person," I said. "But you assumed the worst as usual."

"I didn't feel like this back home," Luca admitted. "You're one of the strongest, most determined people I know, but New York City is far away and you're all alone."

"Bullshit! You track my every move, convinced I'll make a mistake. It's fucking lame."

Luca bit his lower lip. After a few minutes, he asked, "Do you want to break up?"

"I don't know," I replied. "You're shredding my confidence each time you block me."

"It's not a conscious thing," Luca said as if that made it any better.

"I hate being micromanaged," I stated. "Especially by someone who should have complete faith in me. Just because I put on a dress doesn't mean I'm going to run out and get a boob job. Dammit, Luca! I'm not the same person you knew back in the day when I was scribbling hateful graffiti on my tummy with a permanent marker."

Luca chewed on his lower lip until it was raw. In a shaky voice, he asked, "Do you want me to sleep at a hotel tonight?"

"You're not sleeping in my bed, so you should make other arrangements."

Shocked, he whispered, "Do you mean that?"

"What do you think?"

"I've been acting like a jerk," Luca admitted. "You have the right to tell me to fuck off."

"Give me one good reason why I shouldn't."

"We love each other? Please, babe," Luca begged in a low voice. "Don't punish me for being an insensitive pig."

I blinked, surprised to find my lashes were wet. It had been a long and horrible day, and arguing with Luca was the worst part. I could handle most of the drama surrounding Lisa's return, but not without him by my side.

"Chyna?" he prompted. "Will you forgive me?"

I sighed, caving to the inevitable. Any sort of life without Luca was unimaginable. "I already have."

"I swear I'll do better," he said, getting on his knees in front of me. "If you choose to cross-dress indefinitely, I'll be cool with it."

I gave him a half smile. "Don't make statements you can't possibly mean."

"How do you know I won't follow through?"

"I don't for sure, but it'll be nice to see approval on your face, instead of doubt. Clothing shouldn't define a man or woman. It's an enjoyable accessory like anything else."

He made a zipping gesture across his mouth. "No more hateful comments will cross these lips."

"There is one thing you can do," I suggested. "Talk to your football coach and see if they'll take you back. You need an outlet for your nervous energy, and I'd rather it be sports than me."

"Chip said the same thing."

I grinned. "Great minds. It would do you good. We have to learn to function as separate people. Sports have been a part of your life for years. Why stop now? Maybe we won't see each other as often, but there's this wonderful thing called a phone, and Skype sex can be sort of hot. Isolating each other by narrowing our choices isn't love, Luca; it's fear."

"When did you get so damn smart?"

I wiped away the last of my tears and rewarded him with a soft smile. "Is that Luca speak for 'yes, I'll talk to my coach'?"

He nodded, and we held each for several minutes.

"I think we adulted," I joked.

"How's that?"

"Peace and harmony were restored through frank negotiation."

"I love you," Luca said. "So much."

"I love you too," I said. "Never doubt it."

"I promise," Luca said.

We spent several minutes kissing, needing the physical to go hand in hand with our renewed commitment to trust. Gently, he pushed me on my back. Butterflies fluttered in my stomach as Luca slipped his hand underneath the hem of the dress. He paused for a second, stymied by the black tights, but he adjusted quickly and slowly rolled them down my legs. It was a new sensation and added something different to our lovemaking. Once the barriers were lifted, he groped for my cock, and I reached for his zipper, frantically needing to reciprocate.

Luca helped by removing his jeans, and after that, we clung together, lust and love coalescing in one brilliant joining. Each kiss left me wanting more, and the harsh breathing and desperate sounds of need coming from Luca added to my desire. I squirmed, whined, and canted my hips, chasing the approaching orgasm with intent. We came within a few seconds of each other and it had never felt so right.

I picked up the discarded tights and removed my dress, folding it neatly on a chair for court tomorrow. I slipped on a pair of lounging pants and a T-shirt before we rejoined the group in the living room.

Conversation abruptly stopped as soon as we walked in, and everyone seemed to be holding their collective breaths.

"Are you guys okay?" Chip asked Luca.

"Why not ask Chyna," Luca said. "He'll tell you what's going on."

"Can I get you something to drink, sugar?" Alex inquired. "You look like you could use a pick-me-up."

"I'd love some coffee and a sandwich."

"Grilled cheese, okay?"

"Perfect," Chyna said. "Thank you."

Chapter Nineteen

TRYING TO CRAM eight men over six feet tall into my tiny kitchen was a feat, but the dads wouldn't budge, squished together like commuters on a subway. All eyes were on me while I finished my sandwich.

"We should continue this conversation in the living room," I suggested after swallowing the last bite. "It's claustrophobic in here."

"Agreed," Jody replied, heading out of the room with Clark, Grier, Lil, Chip, and Luca following behind. Alex stayed and picked up my plate.

"Go ahead, sugar. I'll clean up and be right out."

"Thank you."

"Sure thing."

In the living room, questions began the minute I walked in. Despite my earlier meltdown, they still focused on my cross-dressing. It was sad they couldn't see the forest for the trees and automatically assumed I'd regressed. Luca was quick to defend me, a gesture I appreciated more than words could say.

"You guys need to chill," he scolded. "Chyna's got this on lockdown."

I smiled at him, acknowledging his support.

"How about telling us what transpired today," Jody said calmly.

"Mom didn't recognize me, Jody. Her confusion was disturbing as hell. I thought a costume change might make a difference."

"And that's all it was to you?" Jody probed. "A change of clothing?"

"Yes."

"You probably think we're overreacting," Jody continued, "but I don't want Lisa to jeopardize your hard-earned stability by triggering a negative response."

I nodded. "Don't read more into this than necessary. I know who I am—one of two sons worrying about his mother."

"Well put," Lil said.

Grier nodded while Clark stayed quiet.

Chip, on the other hand, was clearly upset. "I think it's a mistake to perpetuate Mom's delusions," he warned. "She needs psychiatric help and the first step toward healing is to acknowledge you as her son."

"How can she do that when her reality is completely skewed?" I asked. "Right now she doesn't know up from down."

"I support Chyna's decision," Luca announced. "For whatever it's worth, I'm telling you he's got his act together, and we should stand behind him on this."

"Thank you, Luca."

Alex was unequivocally on my side. "I don't see the harm in wearing a dress if it'll put your mother in a better frame of mind. Her cooperation is essential to her freedom. The authorities won't let you take her out of that place if she's resisting treatment."

Jody acquiesced. "That's true. The officer I spoke with did say she might get away with a fine and a slap on the wrist if she agrees to treatment."

"What exactly are they going to treat her for?" Chip asked.

"They did a blood alcohol test on her after the incident, which is routine for disorderly conduct. Apparently, it was above the legal limit."

"She was drinking too much before she left," Chip informed the group. "I guess it escalated."

"I think it's safe to assume she's an alcoholic and may have abused street drugs as well," Jody stated. "From what I understand, there's something called Manhattan Misdemeanor Treatment Court. It's a program for repeat misdemeanor offenders."

Puzzled, I asked, "Has she been arrested before?"

Jody nodded. "She's been picked up in the past for disorderly conduct and, well, never mind...."

"Soliciting?" Chip asked, ever the realist.

"Allegedly," Jody said kindly.

I felt sick. Then again, wasn't it best to face the truth? How else could Lisa have survived? With no work skills other than the brief stint at Marshalls before the prom, she wasn't equipped to earn a living.

Chip snorted. "She must have failed at that time-honored profession since she's homeless."

Jody scowled at him. "I would keep those remarks to yourself. We don't know the whole story, and it makes you sound like an insensitive fool."

"I'm sorry," Chip said. "That was uncalled for."

"No shit," I seconded, glaring at Chip. Turning back to Jody, I asked, "Tell us about this Misdemeanor Court."

"I only got a brief overview from the officer. Basically, the defendant must agree to enter and stay in a drug or alcohol treatment program. Psyche evaluation and counseling are part of the overall plan. The program includes regular court appearances and supervision by the MMTC judge."

"How come they told you all of this over the phone, and I got no information when I was there?" I bristled with the injustice. I was her son and had a right to know.

"I'm not sure," Jody said, looking apologetic. "Perhaps they thought I'd be better qualified to make decisions as I'm a doctor. It makes a difference."

"That blows."

"Let's move forward from this," Jody said. "We'll have a clearer picture of what's in store for Lisa tomorrow."

Respectfully acknowledging their concerns, I informed the group I planned to go in a dress tomorrow. Lisa's sanity was top priority, and only the familiar might pull her back from the dark place she'd been residing in for so long. What could be more comforting than seeing her twins standing side by side in the courtroom rooting for her? There was no guarantee the deception would work. This afternoon had been a disaster, but now that Chip was in town, I felt more optimistic.

We opted for takeout after the heated discussion and settled on Thai, a family favorite. Lil and Grier perched on the sofa and balanced paper plates on their knees while Clark and Jody remained in the kitchen. The rest of us sat around in a circle on the floor in the living room.

When dinner was over, the 'rents begged off, agreeing to meet in front of the courthouse at nine. They took a cab back to their hotel near Washington Square downtown. Chip decided to stay at the apartment, crashing on the sofa so he could catch up with us while getting to know Alex a little better.

I leaned against Luca, dozing on and off as the guys bullshitted. Chip was grilling Alex in his usual friendly but thorough fashion. This was their first official meeting, and Chip took his brotherly role quite seriously. As such, I didn't bother calling him out for being a nosy jerk. Alex was more than capable of fielding his intrusive questions.

"Hey, bro. Can I interrupt before I fall asleep?"

"Sure," Chip replied.

"If Lisa agrees to enroll in this program, I'd like to be placed on the list of responsible parties. This way, I can visit and be available if they need me."

"Are you sure?" Chip asked.

"Doesn't it make sense? You're too far away and my schedule is more flexible."

"I don't know anything about the law," Chip admitted, "but I'm sure they'll have to follow procedure."

"Dad will never offer," I reminded him, "and I hate to ask Jody and Clark to be responsible. It's not their problem."

"Why don't we wait and see what happens tomorrow," Chip suggested. "There's no sense in getting worked up if things fall into place naturally."

"I want to make sure you back me up if we have choices."

"Only if I think it's good for you."

"Quit it," I warned. "You're not my parent."

"But I'm hardwired to watch your back," Chip argued. "You can't expect me to change overnight."

"For fuck's sake! You and Luca are impossible. It's time to cut the strings, or we're going to do battle each time I make a decision you consider questionable."

Chip glanced at Luca. "Do you agree with him?"

"Hey, I already got my ass kicked today," Luca said. "I'm done being a bodyguard. I'd rather be the guy he loves."

"Good answer," I said, nuzzling Luca's neck.

Chip raised both hands in defeat. "Okay, whatever you say, kiddo."

"We're the same age," I pointed out. "You should stop calling me kiddo."

"What about the whole name changing bit? Is that another one of your great ideas I'm not supposed to question?"

"Don't be such a dick," I said, smarting from the criticism. "The issue of my name was a professional concern, not a whim. After much deliberation, and some friendly advice from people in the industry, I've decided there's nothing wrong with Chyna. It's who I am and people who don't like it can fuck off."

"There are certain advantages to being an only child," Alex interjected in his lazy drawl. "No one will ever disagree with me. Then again, I could have certainly used a brother and friend when I was going through my transition."

Chyna stared at Alex. "Is that your sweet way of telling me I'm being ungrateful?"

"Sugar, that's not for me to decide. All I can say for sure is that I'd soak up the love if I were you. It's a blessing, not a curse."

Way to make it real.

"Am I wrong?" Alex asked.

I shook my head, feeling ashamed. Turning to Chip, I asked, "Will an apology work, or do I need to grovel?"

Chip smirked and gave Alex a thumbs-up.

Luca held me a little tighter and whispered, "We're good."

Alex beamed, apparently happy that peace was restored. "Let's go to bed, or we'll be useless tomorrow."

"Are you coming with us to court?"

"I wish I could, sugar, but I've got a shoot in the morning."

"That's what I thought," I said. "You'll get the scoop when I get home."

"Perfect."

The next morning, I dressed with care, taking the time to shampoo and blow out my hair, applying my makeup with a steady hand.

"You look gorgeous," Luca remarked, coming up from behind. He was staring at our image in the full-length mirror. "I've forgotten how pretty you are dressed up like that."

"Should I do it more often?"

Luca gave a half smile. "Is this another one of your trick questions?"

"No."

"I want you to be happy," Luca said, burying his face in the soft skin between my neck and shoulder.

I turned around and wrapped my arms around Luca's neck. "I know who I am, Luca."

"Anyone I know?"

"Your current boyfriend, future husband, and maybe, if we get lucky, co-parent of a kick-ass little boy."

Luca kissed me. "I'd like a girl as well."

"Let's discuss it when we're ready," I said. "We'll need to find the perfect surrogate."

"In about ten years," Luca smirked. "There's nothing wrong with having a long-range plan."

"That'll give us plenty of time to get our careers up and running so we can afford a family."

"For sure," Luca said. "Kids are expensive."

When we walked out of the bedroom, Chip whistled in appreciation.

"You look fabulous," Alex gushed.

"Thank you," I said, pleased with my appearance. "See you tonight?"

"I'll be here."

We splurged and took a taxi to the courthouse. This time, the reaction to my cross-dressing was more positive. Although they'd seen this very outfit yesterday, they handed out compliments, instead of clucking in disapproval. Lil said I was stylish, and Grier, the interior designer renowned for his color choices, loved the red boots. Jody nodded, acknowledging my presence, but withheld comment. Clark's reaction was straight from the heart.

"We're going to have to keep the guys away with a big stick."

"They'll never get past Chip and me," Luca remarked.

The best reaction of all was when Lisa was led into the courtroom. Someone had made an effort to clean her up today, and even if she was flanked by cops, she didn't look as pitiful. After she was situated with her court-appointed public defender, Lisa got a good look at the people crowding the seats. Her head stopped swiveling back and forth when she spied Chip and me. The blank look of resignation was slowly replaced with a dawning awareness. Without taking her attention off us, she slowly raised her hand and waved.

Chapter Twenty

LISA COOPERATED AS best as could be expected, given her history. She was sentenced to fifteen days in jail and a fine, on the condition she agreed to rehab under the supervision of the Manhattan Misdemeanor Treatment Court. Other than the few minutes I was given to reassure her that I would visit as often as possible, none of us had the opportunity to try to piece together her lost years. It would have to wait.

She kind of lost it at that point, cussing out the cops, judge, and her lawyer in language better suited for the streets. It brought home the stark realization that she was far from sane, despite her scrubbed appearance, and it would take months, if not years, to get her stabilized. The lawyer was quick to point out that public aid would barely cover the cost.

As we were leaving the courthouse, I got a text from Ian. Ignoring Luca's raised eyebrows, I excused myself and found a secluded spot to return the message.

Ian: I'm in a bind

Me: Can I help?

Ian: My model didn't show

Me: You want me instead?

Ian: Please.

Me: How soon?

Ian: Now

Me: Give me 30 minutes

Ian: Thank You!!!

Shit. I hadn't expected payback this early in the game. Was this a legit problem or Ian's way of reminding me that an exchange of favors was in order. I never did tell Luca where I got my outfit, and going into details now might lead to another argument. This wasn't the time to share my concerns about Ian. Luca had been edgy and overprotective ever since this drama with Lisa had started, and I wasn't in a good place either.

There was too much weighing on my mind. Unfortunately, and predictably, Luca sought me out before I could join him.

"What's going on?" he asked, glancing at my phone.

"I have to go to an unexpected photo shoot."

"Can't you put them off until tomorrow?"

"I've already missed several days because of my rash and this crisis with Lisa."

"But I'm going back to Cornell later today," Luca said, trying not to pout.

"There's nothing I can do. I'm sorry, babe."

"Will I see you this weekend?"

"I don't get back from Miami until Saturday."

He frowned.

Gently, I reminded him about last night. "We talked about this."

"Yeah, yeah," he said. "It doesn't mean I have to like it."

"Luca, this is my career and you're being difficult again."

"Are you going home to change first?"

"There's no need."

His eyes narrowed. "You're showing up at a photo shoot in a dress?"

"What's your point?"

"Won't they get the wrong idea?"

"Which idea would you be referring to?"

"Now who's being difficult," he snarled.

My patience, already in short supply, evaporated with his shitty frame of mind. "People in my line of work don't give a damn how I dress as long as I get to work on time. You're so hung up on my attire it's making you stupid."

"Are you ever getting off this soapbox?"

The anger I'd banked last night flared like a raging forest fire. "Get out of my way, Luca."

"Why?" he demanded, blocking my path.

"Because if I stay here for another second, I'll knock your head off."

"What the fuck!"

"Exactly," I said, shouldering past him. I was so done trying to get my point across. I said goodbye to the dads, gave Chip a tight hug, and took a taxi to Ian's studio.

His smile was huge when he opened the door. "You've saving my ass big-time."

"No prob."

"Did everything go well yesterday?" he asked nonchalantly.

I loved that he didn't even blink at my outfit. Granted, every piece had come from his dressing room the day before, but his lack of judgment was refreshing.

"Yes, the camo worked great."

"I'm glad. Family can be such a bitch sometimes."

"No shit." The reminder of Luca's empty promises weighed me down, and Ian must have sensed the immediate shift because he reached for my hand and pulled me inside.

"Let me tell you about this project," he said excitedly as we entered the room where he actually shot the photographs. "I've got this new designer who's catering to a more gender-fluid crowd. He wants his signature model to reflect his mission statement, and he was adamant about finding someone who could wear any of his designs. His original choice bailed for some reason, and I immediately thought of you. I think you'd be perfect."

"So this wouldn't be a one-off?"

"No," Ian said. "If he likes what he sees, you'd sign a one-year contract to represent his line. Melinda can sit down and negotiate the terms, but I can tell you the guy has set aside a huge amount for his campaign, and you would get a large part of it."

I thought about Lisa's upcoming treatment and the lawyer's warning. The cost of good long-term rehab facilities could run into hundreds of thousands. If I wanted her to have the best care, and I did, Medicaid wouldn't foot the bill. Chip didn't have the resources, and I wasn't going to let Jody or Clark shell out more money. They'd given us so much, and asking them to help Lisa felt all kinds of wrong. Even if they could afford it, they shouldn't have to. Ian's offer couldn't have come at a better time.

"I'd be modeling male and fem attire?"

He nodded.

"Prints or runway?"

"Both."

"Why do you want me?"

"Are we in need of an ego stroke, sweetheart?"

"I'm genuinely curious, Ian. There are other more seasoned models who might be better suited for the job."

"And therein lies the problem. They've already been plastered all over the media. My client wants someone so new you're still in the original wrapping. The key words here are fresh, authentic, and unapologetically fluid."

For the longest time, I'd been ashamed of myself, and to hear such praise from a famous man was better than good, it was timely and filled me with hope. For one second, I thought I should run this decision by Luca, but I knew he'd object to seeing me on billboards or print ads in fem garb. His good intentions and reality were still at odds, and I couldn't afford any negative feedback.

"Run this by Melinda first, and if she agrees, I'll do it."

"Fabulous!" Ian said, clapping his hands. "I'll get her on the phone. Meanwhile, get your beautiful self over to makeup and let my ladies work their magic."

I did as directed.

After the makeup artists transformed me into Ian's vision of a trendy Millennial, I was unrecognizable, but pleased with the result. My first outfit consisted of basic skinny jeans, black biker boots, and a red shirt with tiny black buttons on the diagonal. The hand-painted red and black jacket pulled it all together. My hair was piled on my head in a messy knot with several strands falling around my face and covering one eye completely. You couldn't tell if I was male or female, intentional and intriguing. I loved it!

The entire day was one pleasant surprise after another, and I stopped second-guessing Ian after realizing each shot was better than the last. Outfits ranged from the mundane to sublimely fantastical. One minute, I was a badass street kid, and the next, a princess on the lookout for my royal lover. The whole experience—a far cry from our first combative meeting—was a pleasure, and all my misgivings were laid to rest. Ian, at his best, was sweetly affectionate and generous with his praise, but his snarky, demanding flip side showed up whenever a shot didn't go as planned. It had nothing to do with being a good or bad person. This was his artistic style.

When we were done, he kissed my cheek, popped open a bottle of champagne, and poured us two glasses. He was still vibrating from the creative rush, a giddy feeling I couldn't help but share. Positive his client would fall in love with me the minute he laid eyes on the photos, he dialed the guy and urged him to come over as soon as possible. I didn't want to stick around in case there were any concerns he'd want to discuss in private.

On the subway ride home, I melted into the seat, completely drained from the long day. Suddenly, all my doubts about modeling were fading in the wake of this fantastic new offer. Moreover, my concerns over Ian and possible repercussions seemed unfounded. If Luca would get his head out of his ass, I'd feel so much better.

Alex was wonderful when I got in after seven that evening, and he listened with rapt attention as I gave him my news in between scoops of his delicious chili.

"It sounds like this new project is tailor-made for your particular look."

"Right? I'm excited about the potential, but I haven't figured out how I'm going to break the news to Luca."

"Why on earth would he be anything but happy for you?"

"He's having a hard time letting go." Sighing, I added, "The gender-fluid thing is sure to derail him."

"Perhaps he's not the right guy for you after all."

"Wait a second," I protested. "Losing Luca isn't part of my plan."

"Chyna, you have to be realistic," Alex said pragmatically. "You're not the same kid he fell in love with, and if he can't mature at your pace and be the supportive partner you need, then you're better off taking a break until he catches up."

"That's cold."

"I'm sorry you feel that way, but I think it's realistic. People like us can't afford to be around any kind of negativity. Love on someone else's terms isn't my idea of love. Eventually, it'll erode your feelings, and you'll wake up one day and wonder why in hell you wasted all this time with the wrong guy."

I must have looked like I was sucking on a lemon, because Alex immediately grabbed both of my hands and gave me a tight squeeze.

"I'm not saying you should break up, Chyna, but you need to be honest with him. You're not in high school anymore, and there's a lot more at stake than getting kicked off the cheerleading squad. Your future happiness depends on Luca's ability to realize you have a voice, and he needs to listen."

"I honestly think his intentions are good."

"It's obvious that he loves you, but he's working around old assumptions, and his struggle to see life through a different lens will ruin the whole picture."

"He needs to see it through *my* lens."

"Yes."

"I hope you're right."

"Talk to him tonight," Alex suggested. "The longer you put this off, the more difficult it will be."

"I'm beat."

"You're procrastinating," Alex warned.

"I'm afraid to rock the boat."

He stared at me for the longest time before proceeding. "Sugar, your boat is taking on water right now, and you'd better start bailing before you sink. From what you've told me, Luca's life has been smooth sailing up to this point. Even when he came out, there were few obstacles. Your intersex status, and resulting gender dysphoria, must have been troubling when it was revealed. I applaud Luca for standing by you and being a reliable source of support, but your ultimate decision to shed the female and embrace the male fell in step with Luca's wishes. Now you guys are at another crossroads, and he needs to man up or he'll lose you. If he doesn't learn how to make lemonade when life throws him lemons, he'll die of thirst."

I grinned. "We went from sailing analogies to beverages."

Alex chuckled. "Motivational speeches aren't my forte. I'm trying to make this real without sounding like a preacher."

I couldn't help but respond positively. "You've done a fine job so far, Alex. I'll talk to Luca tonight and hopefully get this sorted."

But Luca didn't respond to my text or pick up the phone when I called. Our disagreement had turned into a full-blown rift. My boat was not only rocking, it had capsized.

Chapter Twenty-One

THE SMELL OF fresh coffee, bacon, and eggs, as well as other yeasty aromas, made Luca's stomach rumble. He opened an eye and watched Grier sign the room service receipt while Lil poured the coffee. Luca sat up and stared at the elegant fireplace in the hotel suite. He felt like shit, and probably looked even worse, having fallen asleep on the sofa with all his clothes on immediately after dinner last night.

Conflicted by his argument with Chyna, he'd been reluctant to leave the city yesterday and opted to stay in Manhattan with his fathers. He'd trailed behind them while they shopped Fifth Avenue, sullenly keeping his troubles under wrap, and had declined multiple offers to grab anything that caught his fancy. He knew they were attempting to distract him, and he appreciated the effort, but shopping wasn't the solution.

"Do you mind if we join you?" Lil asked, handing him a cup of joe.

"Hey," Luca said, glancing up. "You wouldn't happen to have an extra toothbrush, would you?"

"I do, but have some coffee first. You look like you need it."

Luca sat up straighter and took a sip. "It's strong."

"Just the way we like it," Lil remarked.

"What's bugging you, kiddo?" Grier asked, smiling good-naturedly. "I didn't want to pry yesterday, but this mopey look is unattractive. Enough already."

"Adulting sucks."

Grier's smile slipped. "That bad?"

"I've made a mess of things at school, and I'm about to lose Chyna. I can't begin to explain how crappy I feel."

"You're obviously miserable."

"I am."

"Why not start at the beginning," Grier prompted.

"You should have stopped me from quitting the team," Luca muttered. "Worst. Decision. Ever."

"We tried, Luca, but you had compelling reasons. Your father and I stopped demanding blind obedience years ago. You're old enough to make your own decisions."

"I know there's no one to blame for this but me."

"Look at the positive, son. They didn't ban you from playing football next year, and they're allowing you to work out with the team, brainstorm with your coaches, watch game videos. That's a step forward."

"But I can't suit up or sit on the sidelines. Officially, I'm off the team."

"Which is only fair. Next time you come up with a harebrained idea, run a few laps to get it out of your system. Snap decisions are usually mistakes."

"I guess."

"There is one advantage to sitting it out," Grier mentioned. "You'll get to come home for Thanksgiving break. I can predict you guys will be tied up next year."

"There's always an upside to everything," Luca admitted dully.

"What's going on with you and Chyna?" Lil probed. "Is it serious?"

Luca hesitated, choosing his words carefully. "I thought he'd appreciate having someone watch his back and shield him from potential harm, but he says I'm micromanaging."

"It's hard to shake old habits," Lil said. "I can remember when Chyna wasn't so self-confident and you were his knight in shining armor."

"Right? Now, all of a sudden, he's questioning anything I say."

"Are you suggesting or demanding?" Grier asked.

Embarrassed, Luca admitted, "A little of both."

Grier shook his head. "Forcing someone to abide by your rules is the kiss of death."

"I don't want to police him, but I love the guy. I can't help worrying."

"Oftentimes people perceive it as meddling," Lil remarked. "You've always been there for Chyna—and everyone you love—which is admirable, until it becomes overbearing. Chyna has been through a lot to get to this point. Major issues none of us have had to deal with, and he's finally starting to become his own person. One he's created, not one he was saddled with by his misguided parents."

"I get all of that, but why does he resent my support when all I've ever wanted to do was protect him?"

"Your situation is unique because Chyna's starting a career while you're still in college. Although you both have learning curves to deal with, living on campus and figuring out your class schedules is far less daunting than trying to rise to the top of a competitive market. In many ways, you're still sheltered while Chyna's out there swimming with the sharks. All his decisions, be they good or bad, are leading toward one goal. Being the best model he can be. As his boyfriend, you can offer your opinion, but in the end, it's not your career on the line."

"What if I don't agree with certain decisions?"

"Can you give us an example?" Grier asked.

"Apparently, I'm judgmental when it comes to cross-dressing in public. Chyna convinced me the dress was necessary to jog Lisa's memory, but yesterday, he went to a modeling shoot straight from court. He practically tore my head off when I suggested he go home to change. Am I wrong in wondering if he's having second thoughts about transitioning?"

"I don't get that vibe, sweetie. I think Chyna is happy with his decision," Lil said.

"Has Chyna said anything to foster these fears, or is this more about your inability to accept someone who's so gender-fluid?" Grier asked.

"Dad," Luca said, sounding offended. "I'm not that kind of guy."

"I don't know, Luca. Your reaction to the dress was a bit extreme."

"I was caught off guard," Luca defended. "If he'd warned me in advance...."

"You'd what? Be more tolerant?" Grier asked, leaning forward. "Will you lose your shit whenever Chyna puts on a skirt? He's in an industry that has little or no boundaries when it comes to attire. I think you need to adjust your mindset."

"Thanks for the support," Luca muttered. "Whose side are you on anyway?"

"The truth," Grier said. "You're in love with a complex guy. Chyna will never fit in a box tied up with a manly blue bow. You've known this for years, Luca. Wasn't it you who said you thought lace underwear was attractive?"

"Under his jeans," Luca corrected. "I never said I'd like it on the outside."

"Does he embarrass you?"

"On the contrary, I couldn't be prouder, but I'm afraid for his safety. Strutting around like a peacock can only lead to trouble."

Grier shook his head. "I'm calling bullshit. If you're unwilling to live with the entire package, you need to be honest and move on. Chyna will never be your typical male. He might have the right genitals, but his psyche was molded by years of conditioning. Wearing a dress is as natural for him as putting on cleats is for you. Can't you see that? This latest costume change was really for Lisa's benefit, but I'm sure it won't be the last time Chyna shows up in fem wear."

"That's another bone we've been picking over like a pair of hyenas," Luca said. "This business with Lisa is driving me crazy. I don't get why Chyna wants to help her after what she did."

"Lisa is his mother and you can't discount that," Grier stated. "Chyna will love her regardless of their turbulent past."

"I don't want Chyna to get hurt again."

"He's beyond Lisa's reach," Grier reminded him.

"You don't think she's got the power to twist Chyna into knots again?"

"Luca, you're disrespecting Chyna by even thinking that's a possibility."

"You don't know Lisa, Dad! She's a manipulative bitch."

"I wouldn't say that in Chyna's presence, or you'll get clobbered."

"Chip says it all the time," Luca protested.

"Chip's grievances with Lisa are bone deep. I'm sure he thinks they're justified, but you aren't entitled to call anyone names like that. I won't allow it," Grier said sternly.

"Fine, I'm sorry for using the B word, but, Dad, Lisa's going to need a lot of help and I know Chyna. He'll offer to contribute financially, which is absolutely unfair. After what Lisa's done to fuck with his head—"

"Language, please."

"Whatever," Luca muttered, ducking his head.

"Look at me," Grier ordered gently.

Luca lifted his gaze.

"The injustice of the situation is frustrating. Lisa purposefully harmed Chyna, and yet she's reaping the benefits of a love she doesn't deserve. In your eyes, you think Chyna should walk away from this sorry mess and never look back. Did I get that right?"

"Yes, but I know it'll never happen."

Grier pulled Luca in for a tight hug. "You're a good person, Luca. No one can fault you for having a big heart, but this is one battle you're never going to win."

"Why can't he see Lisa for the wreck she is?"

"Your boyfriend is a softie when it comes to his mother, and you can't hold that against him. Abusive parents often have the most loyal children. Ask Uncle Clark," Lil advised. "He'll tell you I'm right. Try to see this move as Chyna's way of coming to terms with his past. Getting Lisa the help she needs goes hand in hand with forgiveness."

"I still think it's a mistake."

"And we're back to the original problem," Lil remarked. "You'll lose him if you don't take the necessary steps to see life from his perspective. What's the point in having your way if it'll only make you miserable?"

Luca sniffed, trying to hold back tears, but it was useless. In his heart, he knew his fathers were right. He'd been acting like an opinionated asshole, and shame washed over him, turning him into a hot mess. When did he become the type of man he despised?

"Hey," Grier said, reaching for him. "This isn't the end, you know? It can be the beginning of a long and happy relationship if you take the necessary steps."

"I know," Luca whispered. "Thanks for your help. If I can transfer some of your wisdom into my brain, Chyna and I should be okay."

"Don't be so hard on yourself, Luca. I was an idiot at nineteen," Grier said.

Lil choked on a laugh. "My twenties were one self-inflicted drama after another. I think you're way ahead of the game."

"It doesn't feel that way," Luca said miserably.

"Trust me, sweetie. You are." Lil reached for Luca's hand and tugged. "Come on. Let's close out this pity party and send you on your way."

"Can I at least brush my teeth first?"

"Of course," Grier said, hugging Luca.

He didn't power on his phone until he was at the Cornell Club waiting for the bus. There were several missed calls from Chyna and a few from Zeb. He decided to deal with his roommate first. That was another thing. He'd been too self-absorbed to find out if Zeb needed advice. The more he reflected on his behavior since he'd left home, the less he liked himself. It was time to get his act together, or he'd end up alone.

Zeb sounded concerned when he picked up. "Where are you?"

"Still in Manhattan. I spent the night with my dad's. What's up?"

"Chyna's been calling."

"We had a fight."

"I heard." Zeb sounded sympathetic. "Do you plan on avoiding him indefinitely?"

"I'm not returning his calls until I figure out what I want to say."

"Chyna's leaving for Miami tonight."

"Shit. Are you sure?"

"That's what Alex said."

"About you and Alex…what's going on?"

"Now's not the time, buddy. Call Chyna."

"I think I'll head over to his place."

"Shouldn't you call first?"

"I'll surprise him."

"Are you sure that's a good idea?"

Luca paused. "Unless you know something I don't."

"No, of course not," Zeb said. "It's just that surprises aren't always welcome."

"Whatever," Luca said. "It's easier to talk in person."

He ended the call before Zeb could object and headed toward the subway.

Chapter Twenty-Two

I WAS FILLING my carryall with random shit to take on my trip when the front door buzzed. Bacon went wild, barking and sniffing at the gap between door and floor. I knew it was too early for Alex, and besides, he had a key. If it was a package, they could leave it at the front desk. Which left a service call of some sort, but normally, the property manager would email if anyone had to get into the apartment.

"Who is it?" I asked through the intercom beside the door.

"It's Luca. Let me in, please."

This was unexpected. I'd been calling and texting him all night and been ignored. Now the fool wanted to see me just as I was getting ready to leave town for a few days. Alex probably informed Zeb that I was going to Miami, and when the news reached Luca, he panicked. Typical. Not that I was hiding anything, but I honestly wasn't in the mood to deal with his insecurities. I was still high on my triumphant photo shoot, and sure as shit, he was going to burst my bubble as soon as I explained what my new contract entailed. Because the client had loved the prelims, and paperwork had already been emailed and e-signed, I was committed to Stylize LLC for a year.

Ellis Christopher, the designer and CEO of the company, had sent a huge box of assorted Swiss chocolates—the perfect way to thank me— along with a suitcase filled with his latest designs. I was wearing one of them right then, a knee-length purple jumpsuit with a round neck, long puffy sleeves, and a cinched waist over black leggings. From the front, the outfit was unremarkable, apart from the color, which suited me perfectly, but the open back was held together by one jeweled button and offered a flash of skin whenever I moved. Since my hair was tied up in a loose knot, the special effect would be noticeable the minute I turned around.

I took a deep breath, unlocked the front door, and waited for Luca to step out of the elevator.

Judging from his expression, I could tell my outfit didn't meet his approval. Tough. I was so done trying to make him happy. If he couldn't get behind my career choices, he didn't need to be in my life.

In a subdued voice, he said, "You look...nice."

His lame attempt to say something positive fell flat. He was clearly conflicted, but someone must have knocked some sense into him while we were apart, so...points for trying.

"Thanks, I'm packing. Wanna come in?"

He continued to stare, and I wondered what was going through his head. Was he gearing up for another fight or talking himself off a ledge? It was kind of sad that we were in this place after being in sync throughout high school.

Luca snapped out of his trance and replied, "If I'm not interrupting."

"Nope," I said, pulling the door open so he could pass through.

He picked up Bacon who'd been pawing his pants for attention. "You're leaving for Miami tonight?"

"You must have talked to Zeb."

"Yeah."

"My client can't be put off any longer. Mel's booked me on the ten o'clock flight."

"How long will you be away?"

"A few days."

"Then what?"

"What do you think?" I asked, feeling exasperated. "I'm on to the next job."

"Will that mean more travel?"

"Yes."

He huffed out a breath, visibly annoyed by my standoffish behavior. His cross-examination, camouflaged in stilted politeness, was grating on my last nerve. What did it matter if I was in Manhattan or Maui? Traveling to parts unknown was now a part of my life, and Luca shouldn't expect me to change plans to accommodate his schedule.

"I was hoping we could clear the air between us, but you don't seem receptive," he said.

"Define receptive," I hissed. "If you think I'll fall into your arms because you showed up, guess again."

"I'm trying...to make this right," Luca said haltingly. "I know I overreacted at the courthouse and I'm sorry."

"That's not good enough, Luca. I'm tired of bouncing back and forth between the guy who claims to support me, and his evil twin, the one who's so quick to criticize. Figuring out what's best for my career, while worrying about your reaction, is exhausting. You're either behind me one hundred percent or not at all. And FYI," I continued, knowing I'd be adding fuel to the fire, "I signed a new contract this morning, which involves a lot of cross-dressing. This outfit I'm wearing is one among hundreds I'll be showing off in magazines and on runways."

"I thought we agreed to discuss anything major before arriving at a decision."

"That only works when trust has been established."

"What the hell?" Luca said, stepping closer. "Are you saying you don't trust my judgment anymore?"

"Not when it's clouded by internal conflict! Your biggest fear is that I'll wake up one morning and decide that shedding my female persona was a big mistake."

"Isn't that already happening?" Luca asked. "Look in the mirror, Chyna. I can't see my dude anywhere."

My fist shot out before I could stop myself. I hit Luca on the jaw, and his head snapped back. I was enraged by his insensitive comments, and angry tears were blinding me, but the shock and, yes, utter confusion on his face made the blow worthwhile.

"Did that feel like a girly punch to you?"

Luca touched his chin gingerly and allowed, "That sure as hell didn't, but I've never laid a hand on you before, and I'm not starting now."

"Yeah, well, maybe it's time we get this out of our system. Go ahead," I dared. "Hit me!"

Luca didn't move.

I shoved his chest with both hands, and he took a step back but didn't topple. He was used to being manhandled on the football field, far better trained at the physical aspects of fighting than I'd ever be. Still, I had surprise on my side, and weeks of bottled up anger. I drove into him and literally moved us across the room. We slammed into the wall, and I pummeled him with all the force I could muster. He grunted in pain but didn't retaliate. My puny attempt to knock him down didn't work, and the frustration boiled over making me flail blindly.

Gripping my arms, Luca bellowed, "Stop it."

"Not on your life," I retaliated.

Our faces were inches away from each other and we were both shaking with pent-up fury, but he wouldn't rise to the bait.

"I'm not fighting you," he snarled, hot breath ghosting over me. Bright spots of color bloomed on his cheekbones, and his eyes glittered, but he didn't waver. "Calm the fuck down and talk to me."

"You're a controlling piece of shit!"

"I know," Luca agreed. "I've made a lot of mistakes since we left home."

The admission brought me up short. My anger slowly drained out of me, but I had to get my point across before I lost my nerve.

"Listen to me," I insisted. "You keep calling me your boyfriend, and you sure as shit have no problem sucking my cock, but when it comes to making decisions about my life as a whole, you treat me like I'm the same conflicted girl in a training bra. Why is that, Luca? Don't I deserve the same respect you give Chip?"

Luca lowered his eyes.

"Answer me!"

He shook his head, seemingly at a loss for words. Stymied by this passive response, I considered another approach. Should I put my fist through the wall or fuck the shit out of him? What could I do to prove I wasn't the porcelain doll he'd been humoring for years?

"Don't you think I want to get past this, too?" he asked suddenly.

"You're all talk," I accused. "You give me zero credit unless I force it out of you."

"Punching my lights out isn't the way to solve this. Dammit, Chyna." He rubbed his chin. "Way to uppercut. Who taught you to box?"

"I've been lifting weights and using Chip's punching bag on and off since I was outed."

"Why didn't you tell me?"

"I dunno," I spluttered. "Maybe because you weren't ready to let go of your baby doll."

"That's not fair," he objected. "I've supported all your decisions."

"Yeah, Luca, on the surface. You keep saying you want a boyfriend, but all this time, you've been treating me like Chip's sister, the one who trailed behind you guys for years. How fucked up is that?"

Luca let out a loud sigh and sank to the floor. He wrapped his arms around his knees and lowered his head. "I've been such a dumbass."

I slumped down beside him and also hugged my legs close to my chest.

"Are you breaking up with me?" Luca asked in a muffled voice.

"Do you want to?"

"No!"

We lifted our heads at the same time and turned toward each other. Luca appeared as wrecked on the outside as I felt inside. His lower lip was swollen from where I'd grazed it, and an ugly bruise was starting to form on his jaw. I regretted using force, but words had failed to penetrate his thick skull whereas a blow on the chin appeared to have accomplished the impossible. He was looking at me with a new measure of respect.

Groping for his hand, I meshed fingers with him, and I tried to explain my feelings with far less rancor.

"I love you, but you'll lose me if you don't accept me for who I am. Makeup and frilly clothes are my jam. When photogs fawn over me, I soak it up. I love the attention as much, if not more, than your garden-variety model. All my life, I've been missing out in one way or the other, but now I'm finally coming into my own. I can't be with someone who doesn't get me. I'm a man, notwithstanding my love for feminine attire, and I don't know how else to prove my point. You have to get past your misconceptions regarding my past. I'll be shattered if you choose to walk away, but I won't hold it against you. This has to be right for both of us."

"You and I are meant to be together," Luca stated. "That's a given. I knew it back in high school, and my love for you has never wavered. But there's a side of me—a big part of me, actually—that feels responsible for your safety. It stems from watching you struggle with your gender issues, as well as the bullying you endured, and then finding out how Lisa fucked with your head. All this combined with the physical distance compels me to treat you differently from Chip or other guys I might know. I'm aware that it's irrational, and being bossy and overbearing will only push you away. I don't blame you in the least for wanting to knock my head off. If the roles were reversed, I would have set you straight long ago, except I'm the one in need of help. My fucking emotions are screwing up my good sense. Why can't I wrap you up in a protective bubble and keep you by my side forever?"

"Because it's not necessary," I reminded him. "I'm not the same person anymore and neither are you."

"Maybe so, but I can't curb my vivid imagination. That scene at the prom keeps replaying in my head. I honestly feel the main reason I object to your cross-dressing in public is not because I'm ashamed of you, or you'll start questioning your gender, but I'm worried you'll be attacked by some right-wing psycho for no good reason. You've seen the headlines. What makes you think you'll be exempt?"

"Didn't I just prove I can take care of myself?"

Luca snorted. "I had no idea I was dating a welterweight."

"Yeah, you'd better watch it."

"Okay, I'll admit you can handle yourself in a fight, but what if there's more than one person? Or if they have a gun?"

"As much as I consider you a superhero, even you can't stop a bullet," I pointed out. "If someone is intent on killing me, they'll succeed."

"You're not helping at all," Luca muttered. "Are you certain about this new contract? You don't think it'll put you at risk? What about security? Will you have someone watching your back during public appearances? The political climate sucks at the moment, and hate crimes are on the rise. And that's not me being overly cautious; it's reality."

"I'm sure the people behind this campaign will do everything in their power to keep me safe. They're not oblivious to what's happening out there, but trends are what make the industry, and at the moment, I'm a moneymaker. The haters won't go away regardless of what I wear, so why should we cave to their threats? You need to take a chill pill and quit worrying."

Luca sighed.

It wasn't the rousing endorsement I was hoping for, but he seemed more compliant. With that in mind, I prompted, "Is there anything else you'd like to address now that we're being completely honest?"

"How do you plan to handle Lisa's rehabilitation?"

"What do you mean?"

"The lawyer said it would cost a bundle."

"You won't have to pay for it," I said defensively. "Lisa's treatment was on my mind when I considered this new contract."

"So you are planning to foot the bill?"

"Right now, I have no idea what's in store for her or how much it'll cost. The only thing I know for certain is that she'll need help."

"And you've chosen to pitch in," Luca complained. "Why not walk away?"

"That would be the easiest solution, but my conscience won't allow it."

"My dad's said the same thing," Luca admitted. "They told me to butt out."

I was surprised but relieved. "Take the advice, Luca. Don't make me choose."

There was nothing more to say after that. I got off the floor and headed for the bathroom to try to repair my makeup. Luca followed quietly and watched as I fussed with my face.

"You look fine, babe."

"My mess will wash off, but you need an ice pack on your chin."

"I'm not worried about it."

Putting down the washcloth, I reached out, "Luca?"

"What, babe?"

"I'm sorry for hitting you."

"Don't be," he said quickly. "I deserved it."

"Violence is never the answer."

"You're right, but in this case, I think you had no other choice. Some of the shit I've said and done...." His words trailed off and he lowered his gaze.

"Do you mean it?"

He nodded. "Instead of learning how to cope with our new situation and change up my moves like a seasoned player, I've been stuck in a rut, running the same old patterns even when they're no longer working."

"Way to make this about football."

He looked up, and there were fresh tears on his cheeks. "I know we're talking about our lives, but the analogy applies. I've lost sight of the goal, and it was high time you showed me exactly how you feel."

"If you really mean that, I forgive you."

Luca moved closer, wrapping his arms loosely around my waist. "I do. Is it okay if I kiss you?"

I nodded and opened up to him when he pressed his lips against mine. We shuffled our way from the bathroom to the bedroom, refusing to let go of each other in case it would stop the momentum. After the last thirty-six hours, I couldn't bear to leave for Miami without renewing our commitment in the most basic way.

We fumbled with zippers and buttons, and his clothes fell away in minutes, while my outfit tested Luca's patience.

"Don't rip it off," I warned as he struggled with the silk. "There will be hell to pay if you do."

"Another reason to wear nothing when I'm around," Luca teased.

I couldn't help but laugh at his logic. Finally, when the last layer was eliminated, and we lay chest to chest, rubbing our cocks frantically against each other, my brain did a quick reboot and I flipped us over. With Luca on the bottom, I positioned my hands on his knees and pushed his legs up to his chest.

"Babe?" he asked, eyes wide.

Luca hardly ever bottomed, and for the most part, I was okay with it. But not tonight. The demon that had taken over my brain cells earlier demanded I top, reminding Luca in no uncertain terms that I might be wearing eye shadow and mascara, but I was a man in every sense of the word.

"I'm going to fuck you so hard you'll think of me long after I board that plane."

Luca flushed and he reached up and thumbed my lower lip. In a sultry voice, he asked, "Got lube?"

I'd expected a little resistance, his usual attempt to take charge, instead of this complete and absolute surrender. I felt something close to euphoric as I imagined him lying on my bed with cum dribbling out of him while I zoomed off to Miami. The tiny packet of lube was underneath my pillow where I usually stashed it, and I slicked us up with a shaky hand. I was so hot for him I was sure I'd nut before I even got past his tight ring.

I gritted my teeth and moaned as I buried my cock in his ass, loving the sound of Luca's grunt, a combination of surprise and even a little pain, always a part of this experience. I worked myself deeper into his core, thrusting in and out with precision until I felt him go rigid when I brushed his prostate.

"Right there," he panted. "Keep going."

And I did. Plowing him with determination, intent on leaving a tangible reminder that he was mine and we were in this for the long haul. We'd stay the course and learn how to dodge the fear and insecurity. There were years ahead of us, plenty of time to get things sorted out. It would take more than one discussion to set things right—even if we had to duke it out a few more times—but our love was worth fighting for, and as long as we made the effort, we'd be okay.

Chapter Twenty-Three

I'D FALLEN INTO a pattern of visiting Lisa every other weekend, and when Luca was in town, he usually accompanied me. Narco Freedom Inc, a long-term rehab facility in the Bronx, was one of the few places that accepted court-appointed Medicaid patients. Lisa fit the criteria, and although it was a hike and a half and my out of pocket expenses were a small fortune, we'd heard good things about the place.

Initially, Chip and Luca were of the opinion that I should limit my visits. Why expend emotional energy on someone whose grasp on reality was so tentative? I told them to mind their own business and insisted she'd never recover even a part of her former self if I walked away at this juncture.

What I'd gathered from the doctors, was that her decline started years ago. Women afflicted with drug or alcohol addictions developed their problems as a means of coping with trauma and emotional pain. In Lisa's case, the pressure began when she first realized she couldn't conceive a child naturally. The stress of multiple in vitro attempts, compounded by her decision to raise her outwardly male intersex child as female, and the subsequent desertion (and divorce) by a man who should have, by all rights, remained at her side, eroded what little stability she had left.

The ugly details of her perilous slide from ordinary suburbanite to unstable wanderer came out in fits and starts. She'd hooked up with a trucker the night she walked away from us, hitchhiking off Route 14 at nine o'clock in the evening. With no money in her purse, all Lisa had to trade was sex.

Her increasing use of alcohol and lack of funds were the perfect combination to make Lisa a compliant bitch while the trucker crisscrossed the country. Using the man's phone, she kept tabs on us by lurking on our social media sites. By the time we'd graduated high school, and I was on my way to New York to start a modeling career, Lisa was ready for a change as well. She slipped away outside Buffalo, New York, taking whatever money she could find for a bus ticket to Manhattan.

Having burnt her bridges in such a spectacular fashion, she couldn't show up at my apartment expecting a hero's welcome. As days turned into weeks, and then months, Lisa's tentative grasp on reality disappeared and survival instincts kicked in. At first, she peddled her body for food and shelter, but when that stopped working, she began scavenging for recyclables.

Now that time had passed and I was in a much better place, I could view Lisa's behavior from an adult's perspective. Her downfall had been inevitable. There was no reason to feel guilty for shoving her out of my mind the moment she disappeared. We'd both made choices, a lot of good ones in my case, and mostly bad in hers, but the worst was over. Now we could concentrate on the future, and getting Lisa the help she needed was the first step.

Although a lot of her daily expenses were covered, I paid for specialized one-on-one psychiatric help. Unscrambling Lisa's past to give her a viable future was a tedious, time-consuming, and costly process that might take months, if not years. She had selective amnesia, in my opinion, pushing away the ugly events while hanging on to the highlights of her life possessively. One minute, she'd recognize me, and then, just as quickly, would forget my name and call me Chip. I could deal with her lapses, if we moved in the right direction. In the event she couldn't be rehabilitated socially, we'd have to reevaluate.

Luca was also working on his compassion. He continued to feel it was intrinsically wrong to give Lisa a hand after everything she'd done to ruin my life, but Zeb, along with Grier and Lil, advised restraint. They kept reminding him that making me choose between our relationship and my mother would be a huge mistake. As a constant in Luca's daily life, Zeb turned out to be the perfect sounding board, keeping him grounded whenever he came close to going off the rails.

Chip had promised to keep in touch by phone or visit if and when he could get away. It was the most I could ask for, and my only hope was that he'd follow through. So far, he hadn't stepped foot in the place.

Today was one of Lisa's good days. She recognized Luca and me when we walked in and didn't make any snide comments—apart from the usual fashion critique associated with my decidedly male attire. Today, I was wearing ripped jeans, a weathered leather jacket, and a backward-facing ball cap.

"If you insist on being a guy, a more preppy look will go a long way to win me over," Lisa said tersely. "Honestly, Chyna. Where do you buy your clothes?"

I laughed. "If you had any idea how much this outfit cost, you wouldn't be so critical."

"Why? Is that awful jacket expensive?"

"It's a Christopher original."

"So?"

I rolled my eyes, and Luca intervened. "High fashion, Mrs. Davidson, and pricey."

"He looks like an out-of-work rocker," Lisa said derisively. "And the hair? Smooshed flat by that awful cap."

"I like it," Luca said.

She gave Luca a withering look. He was getting better at keeping his cool rather than engaging her in useless arguments. There was no changing Lisa's mind when it came to my gender. She was convinced I would have transitioned to female without a problem if Luca hadn't been in the picture. It was much easier to blame him for "turning" me into a boy rather than admit she was wrong. It was ludicrous but par for the course, according to the docs. She wasn't capable of accepting responsibility for any of her actions.

Ignoring him, Lisa turned toward me, and asked, "Do you ever wear suits and ties?"

"Of course I do," I said patiently. "I model for the finest designers in the world, but on the weekends, I want to chill."

"And that involves ratty jeans and jackets that look like they've seen better days?"

"That's right," I replied with a smirk. "How was your week?"

Perking up slightly, Lisa said, "I'm learning how to type on the computer."

"That's great," Luca interjected.

"My doctor said by the time I'm ready to leave, I'll be able to get a real job."

Luca smiled encouragingly. "Good times."

"And the alcohol cravings?" I asked pointedly.

Lisa frowned.

"Still bad?"

"Let's talk about something more pleasant," Lisa deflected.

We chatted about TV shows and movie stars as if it was the most normal thing in the world, and we weren't in a communal area at a drug and alcohol rehabilitation facility. Once again, Lisa asked about my job and I responded, repeating the same information I shared each time I visited. Aside from missing huge gaps in her past, Lisa also suffered from short-term memory loss. I often wondered if she was getting Alzheimer's, but the doctors said it was a combination of her addictions, along with avoidance. Whatever the reason, she pressed for details, living vicariously off my life as a model.

My collaboration with Stylize was a great success. Ian's photographs had set the stage, and a few runway appearances had locked in my role as the new spokesperson for the company. I was starting to get a following on social media, and I'd appeared briefly on Entertainment Tonight and TMZ as the trendy fashionista creating a buzz. It drove Luca insane when they speculated on my love life, and he urged me to tell them I was in a relationship, but Mel advised against it. It was better to keep them guessing so my name stayed in the spotlight. After reflecting on the pros and cons, I decided Luca was more important than public opinion. I let everyone know I was firmly committed to an aspiring architect who could easily pass for a model if he ever changed career. The look of pure joy on Luca's face when we watched my taped interview on *The Talk* more than made up for Mel's disapproval.

We were leaving for Grand Turk Island that afternoon to spend Christmas with the entire family—Luca's dads, my foster fathers, Chip, and his girlfriend, Meghan. Missing were Zeb and Alex, now considered members of our extended family. They'd opted to stay in Manhattan to continue exploring their relationship, which had gone from zero to intense in the span of three months. Having the apartment to themselves was almost as good as flying away to some exotic island. That could wait for another holiday, Zeb assured Luca after the invitation was extended.

For someone who'd been so reticent about his sexuality when he first landed at Cornell, Zeb was embracing his new normal and plying Luca with questions on the daily. Alex was far more private, but I could tell he was thrilled by the prospect of having Zeb as his guest for an entire week.

On the cab ride to the airport, Luca and I chatted about the future of our roommates. Would they make it as a couple, or not? They had their own set of challenges, not insurmountable in my opinion, but noteworthy, according to Luca. Zeb's family was staunchly Catholic and had no idea Zeb was in a same-sex relationship—with a transgender man. It shouldn't make a difference whether Alex was cis or not, it certainly didn't to Zeb, but Luca predicted fireworks when the Filipino relatives came for a visit. Fortunately, that wasn't on the books yet.

Because we had the coolest parents on the planet, Luca and I were able to stay in the same room at the Sandal's resort they'd booked months ago. As were Chip and Meghan. Having been raised by a single mom, I'd never had the advantage of seeing a good relationship in progress. It was only since Chip and I were fostered that we got a taste of marriage at its finest.

Lil and Grier, Luca's parents, had hooked up when Luca was six, tied the knot a few years later, and had remained deeply in love. They hardly ever argued, and when they did, it was brief and usually ended in laughter with copious amounts of hugs and kisses.

Clark and Jody, our foster fathers, were another story. From the little I'd gathered, Clark had been deeply closeted when he was playing college football, but he'd come out for Jody, the doctor who'd treated him after he broke his arm. In an age when football players would rather die than reveal their orientation, Clark had announced his love for Jody on national TV shortly before he was drafted into the NFL. It was the stuff of legends and inspiring to men and women alike. I was in awe of their courage and continued commitment to each other. After being a part of my father and mother's disastrous pairing, my belief in the sacrament of marriage had taken a severe hit, but it was renewed whenever I watched the two couples interact.

Our days were usually spent indulging in one water sport after another. I'd tried snorkeling, fishing, scuba diving, waterskiing, and parasailing. The four of us—Luca, Chip, Meghan, and I—were more inclined to the physical side of vacationing while the older guys were content lounging by the pool or being pampered by the amazing staff with heavenly massages on tables overlooking the ocean. Umbrella drinks were always within reach, and snacks were plentiful.

We shared evening meals, crowding around a large candlelit table, recounting the day's events while a Mariachi band played softly in the background. The last three months had been a bitch, and I was done with indecision and drama. Luca was learning how to live with my constant traveling, having taken up yoga to relieve some of the stress that tended to accumulate when he let his imagination run wild. Once he was officially back on the football team and had a legit outlet for his nervous energy, I was certain his state of mind would improve even further.

I spent as much time with him as possible, either at my place or in Ithaca at a nice B and B, and his bouts of jealousy were less frequent. Learning to trust each other's judgment was the most difficult part of our relationship, but we were getting there. We lived for weeks like this, when we could put school and career on hold and get back to basics—sex, fun, and more sex. Preferably in that order.

Chip shocked us on our last night by proposing to Meghan. Somehow, he'd managed to come up with the money for a decent-size diamond. With the collaboration of Lil, an inveterate romantic, he had the maître d' stuff the engagement ring into a tub of guacamole, which Meghan fished out with a tortilla chip. It wasn't the most inspired choice, but it was typical of Chip, a no-nonsense man of science. When Meghan started to cry, I followed, and pretty soon the entire group was laugh/sniffing and toasting their happiness with bathtub-size margaritas. We got drunk that night and danced until the wee hours. Toward dawn, we made our way to the beach to watch the sun rise. It was a perfect end to a fabulous vacation.

On the plane ride back to New York City, Luca and I snuggled under a blanket and pledged our love for the hundredth time in as many days. To my surprise, he slipped a silver band on my ring finger.

"I'm hoping we can get formally engaged sometime next year, but for now, will you accept this commitment ring?"

"I'd love to," I said, sealing my decision with a soft kiss. "Did you buy a match for yourself?"

He smiled happily and handed it over, so I could place it on his finger. I'd been contemplating the idea of quitting modeling once my contract with Stylize expired. I'd grown to love my new career, but I also knew it was transient. I'd always intended to get my degree in interior design, and I was determined to spend the rest of my life working with Luca at his father's architectural firm. Having been surrounded by such inspiring role models this week made it easier to envision a life that didn't involve being in the spotlight.

I wasn't planning on saying anything until I was certain, but his proposal was the push I needed to share my thoughts. Not surprisingly, he cried when I told him I intended to join him at Cornell next fall.

"Are you sure?" he asked, wiping his tears on his sleeve. "You're giving up a lot."

"I plan on amassing a small fortune before I quit."

"Anyone can be an interior designer, but a supermodel? Come on, babe. You should milk this while you can."

"I know, but I've been recalling my conversation with Ian at the dance club when I asked him if the bullshit was worth it. Modeling was a great idea back in the day when I wasn't sure who or what I was supposed to be. After hiding in the shadows for so long, being worshipped by photogs and fashion designers is the ultimate validation. Conversely, the reality, as it pertains to me, is far from satisfying. My face and body are a genetic gift that requires little effort after it's all said and done. I want to work in a field where I can be mentally stimulated by creating beautiful and sustainable environments for homes and businesses. Being a part of your fathers' firm, working with you by my side, sharing a life doing what we love, are more important than a hefty bank account and constant accolades."

"You don't think it's worth it?"

I shook my head. "Not by a long shot."

"Maybe you can do it part-time while you're earning your degree?"

"The extra dough would give us a nice nest egg," I agreed. "It's something to consider."

We got back to Manhattan at noon, in plenty of time for Luca to catch the five o'clock bus to Cornell.

"You want to grab a bite before you go?" I asked. "We can have the cab drop us off at that hamburger place close to the Club."

"That sounds great," Luca said. "I'm famished."

When we walked into P.J. Clarke's, we were excited to see that Zeb and Alex had the same idea. Heading straight for their table, we exchanged greetings and bro hugs.

"Did you guys just fly in?" Zeb asked.

"Yup, and when Chyna suggested food, I jumped on the idea. It's easier to sleep on the bus if I don't have to listen to my stomach growling," Luca joked.

"Have a good vacay?" Alex asked.

"It was great," Chyna said. "How was yours?"

Zeb and Alex looked at each other, holding the stare for a few beats until I couldn't stand it. "Okay, you need not reply. I can smell the sex oozing off you guys."

"We took a shower," Zeb protested indignantly.

When Alex stopped laughing, he asked, "What was the highlight of your trip?"

"Chip asked Meghan to marry him," I said excitedly. "It's was totes romantic."

"Did she say yes?"

"Of course," Luca said. "They're getting hitched next summer. A location wedding somewhere in the Caribbean. The 'rents will cover the cost and asked us to join them for a week."

"So Zeb and I will have the apartment to ourselves again?" Alex asked, looking radiant.

"Unless you want to come to the wedding."

"No, thanks," Alex replied. "I won't kennel Bacon."

"Most airlines allow dogs in the cabin," Luca remarked. "You want me to look into it?"

"Nope," Zeb interjected decisively.

I watched my roommate communicating silently with Luca's roommate. It was another affirmation that a heart and mind in sync could overcome whatever obstacles were thrown in its path. These two were definitely on the right track.

I took a bite of my hamburger and sighed contentedly. We'd subsisted on fresh seafood for a week, and it had been out of this world, but there was nothing like a juicy burger that screamed home. It was good to be back.

About the Author

Mickie B. Ashling is the pseudonym of a multifaceted woman who is a product of her upbringing in multiple cultures, having lived in Japan, the Philippines, Spain, the Middle East, and the USA. Fluent in three languages, she's a citizen of the world and an interesting mixture of East and West. A little bit of this and a lot of that have brought a unique touch to her literary voice she could never learn from textbooks.

By the time Mickie discovered her talent for writing, real life got in the way, and the business of raising four sons took priority. With the advent of e-publishing—and the inevitable emptying nest—dreams of becoming a published writer were resurrected and she's never looked back.

She stumbled into the world of men who love men in 2002 and continues to draw inspiration from their ongoing struggle to find equality and happiness in this oftentimes skewed and intolerant world. Her award-winning novels have been called "gut-wrenching, daring, and thought-provoking." She admits to being an angst queen and making her men work damn hard for their happy endings.

Email: www.mickie.ashling@gmail.com

Website: www.mickieashling.com

Blog: www.mickiebashling.blogspot.com

Facebook: www.facebook.com/mickie.ashling

Twitter: @MickieAshling

Also by Mickie B. Ashling

Third Son

Also Available from NineStar Press

Connect with NineStar Press

www.ninestarpress.com

www.facebook.com/ninestarpress

www.facebook.com/groups/NineStarNiche

www.twitter.com/ninestarpress

www.tumblr.com/blog/ninestarpress

www.ingramcontent.com/pod-product-compliance
Lightning Source LLC
Chambersburg PA
CBHW060604190726
48283CB00003B/1151